The Mystery of the Pale King

Sam Flynn

Timber Ghost Press

The Mystery of the Pale King

Copyright © 2024, Sam Flynn, Timber Ghost Press

Published by Timber Ghost Press

Printed in the United States of America

Edited by: Beverly Bernard

Cover Art and Design by: Greg Chapman

Interior Design: Timber Ghost Press

Print ISBN: 979-8-9883040-6-7

www.TimberGhostPress.com

Contents

For Frodo

Part I

The Journey

The Sol Church's record of the events in Hathur, or rather the remnants I managed to rescue from the ruins of the Holy City, reads, "*The resurgence of suppressed beliefs in Yorgos, and the rebellions incited by their malignancy, can be directly traced back to the death of the Hero of Hathur, whose storied life ended in tragedy when the living saint was murdered by one of our very own priests, the turncloak Bishop Antonius ...*"

Lies upon lies upon lies. To think, I once dreamt of being a priest.

Even with a soul calloused by many betrayals, the depth of erasure committed by the institution to which I had dedicated my life still wounds me. It cannot, it should not, but it does. I shall not allow their final slander to remain buried. I must write for the sake of those who died and yet more for those who live so that the truth of what happened in Hathur may not be forgotten. I do not know of any person alive, myself included, who could explain what truly occurred in that haunted domain. As much as I would like, I cannot promise answers. Only my truth. There are enough lies in the world and, as you shall come to understand, I have no desire to tell more. I know only that I *must* record, as best as I can, that which defies description.

———————◆○◆———————

Bishop Antonius ... a wolf clothed as a shepherd, a pagan fanatic of the worst sort, a demon-worshipper who also killed the Hero's three grown children. The Church bears no responsibility for the sins committed by such a duplicitous soul.

-From the official records of the Sol Church, dictated by Archbishop Claudius

———————◆○◆———————

Over two-score soldiers and sailors accompanied us from the Holy City across the starving kingdom of Yorgos, the most the Archbishop claimed the Church could spare amid famine and unrest. Our mission was simple: deliver the royal edict declaring the Church's repossession of the southern border province of Hathur to the legendary "Hero of Hathur."

"An important clerical duty," Archbishop Claudius promised Bishop Antonius, to whom I was assigned as page, going where he went, attending to his needs, and recording his dictations. Menial as my tasks were, I was proud of my post. Bishop—as he insisted I solely refer to him—was remarkably young for his position and many, including myself, wondered of his potential ambitions, but unlike the previous Bishops I had served, lust and sin had not replaced his devotion to the light of the Sol Creator. Far from power-hungry,

Bishop was a reluctant and pious leader more at home preaching to the poor peasantry than cajoling the wealthier circles he often had to navigate, many of whom knew him as the priest who wished to allow women entry into the Holy City for the first time in centuries, the stance which made me admire him most.

I must confess to foolish surprise when the Archbishop called us to his solarium, an opulent golden room larger than most of the city's chapels, and first told us of the mission. Whatever rumors of jealousy within the Church over the Hero's popularity, I never believed the priesthood would act against one of its living saints. My maturation since I joined the Church three years previous could not erase my roots in legends I had grown up hearing about the Hero, Cassius Hathur. All of Yorgos knew him as one of the kingdom's greatest men, who led conquest of the outer lands, bearing the One and Only banner of the blazing sun, ten fiery orange tendrils extending from the yellow circle. As a reward for his successful mission, the Church bequeathed him the distant-but-bountiful border province of Hathur.

My expectations of a meeting between Bishop and Archbishop Claudius were high. Imagine my shock when the Archbishop confided the reason he summoned us: the Hero of Hathur had brought his eponymous province to bankruptcy.

"The Church did not know how dire the situation was until the lord's three children Drusus, Livia, and Julius appealed to the Holy City," he explained. "They revealed that Lord Hathur has sold so much land, he no longer has the collateral to cover his enormous debts. The king granted their request for an edict that forbids further property sales, as well as declaring his Church credit frozen and his remaining estates forfeit." He handed over a piece of parchment.

"My economic knowledge is limited," Bishop hedged as he read, "but if he exhausted his estates and borrowed on top of the sales, the coinage had to go somewhere. What extravagance was worth all this land and loans?"

The Archbishop sighed deeply before answering. "A play."

Bishop's astonishment left him blank-faced and blinking. The benefit—or burden—of hindsight makes me suspect he paused not from astonishment but creeping dread. He regained focus, cleared his throat, and smiled weakly. "I hope it's a farce about a bankrupt lord."

The Archbishop wrinkled his nose. "Decidedly not. Lord Hathur not only wrote but performs the titular lead role in this play of his, '*The Mystery of the Pale King*.'"

My quill scratched and I looked up, certain at the time I'd misheard. Bishop's eyes flicked over to me briefly.

"And far from farce," the Archbishop continued, oblivious, "travelers' tales of the performances describe nothing less than *pagan heresy*. Blasphemy denigrating the Sol Creator as a false god and our Church's charitable record of proselytizing our faith in conquered lands like Hathur. He refused his children's pleas to halt his nightly performances. Moreover, in this time of famine, he has opened up his cellars and storehouses to the peasants. Smallfolk across Yorgos flock to Hathur to partake of the free food and drink provided for his profane spectacle!"

"My page might know about this heresy. He was born in Hathur, grew up there." Bishop twisted in his chair to face me. "Faron, have you heard of this Pale King?"

The Archbishop raised an eyebrow. I swallowed, taking the time to put down my quill before speaking. "Yes, I have. It concerns—"

"I don't need a page to define heresy for me," he harrumphed and readjusted in his chair.

In truth, I was relieved not to speak and flattered by the comparison, but Bishop seemed affronted. "You must have more than travelers' tales to charge the Hero of heresy," he said.

The Archbishop's lips were white lines. "Details come from the dispatches of our first messenger, Cleric Paulus. He went missing after his arrival in Hathur. His final missive was partially destroyed, the surviving contents nigh incoherent, save the last sentences."

The Archbishop permitted us to view Paulus' half-burnt letter, the only legible words of which I reproduce here: *The Creator is a lie. We are not light but shadow. The darkness is not empty. Do not come looking for me. Do not come at all.*

Bishop was perturbed. "I know Paulus well. The Creator blessed him with a cleverness I envy. The missive could be bait, written under duress, or perhaps coded."

"Whatever Cleric Paulus' fate, the letter is more proof that Lord Hathur's heretical self-aggrandizement spreads like a sickness. The Church won't stand for his apostasy any longer. You shall sail the Queen's River south to Hathur and put an end to it."

At that point, he ordered me to stop recording. I did then, but I shall do no such thing now.

"One final item." The Archbishop withdrew a scroll from his sleeve and handed it to Bishop, who broke the seal and read. By the time he finished, his eye started twitching, a tic both unusual and distressing. Then he stood from his seat, walked to the fireplace, and tossed the parchment to the flames. A snap and a flash, and the scroll became smoke—but the message lingered. I would find out later what it contained, but in the moment, baffled was all I could be.

Bishop stared at the fire. "Why does King Leo ask this of me?"

"His price for the Church's repossession of Hathur."

"This is why I was given the Bishopric so quickly, isn't it? It was never about merit."

The Archbishop frowned but allowed his idealistic impertinence to slide. "When you return, the king shall make you an Archbishop. Consider this mission simply a steppingstone."

"'A steppingstone.'" He chuckled humorlessly. "I thought I could escape here."

"None of us can escape the design of our Sol Creator," the Archbishop preached. "Not even the Hero of Hathur."

I had to process the bitter implosion of a foundational childhood legend while my superiors spoke in notes, riddles, and lamentations. During preparations for our journey to the outlands, my resentment was high. Why would the Hero shame himself and the Creator? How could the Creator have allowed this debacle? I thought about the secret scroll and Bishop's reaction. Resentment, just like me. He did not like what was asked of him any more than I did.

The more I pondered, the more convinced I became that King Leo was jealous of the Hero, jealous that other nobles called him the true king of Yorgos, jealous that smallfolk worshipped his benevolence instead of the Church's, a prophet outside their control. That, I suspected, was the true reason for the Archbishop's ire.

What a fool I was.

I was blind. Blind to the spider's web I was caught in. Blind to the pain ahead. Every inch of my body yearns to reach back in time and save myself from the coming horror. Yet, if I could intervene in the past, I know I would not listen, even to myself. I would plunge ahead, insistent that I was different, my dedication to, and ambition within, the Church ironclad, my faith in the Sol Creator unshakable. I had the worst affliction of all: I believed I was right.

Bishop, on the other hand, displayed doubt for the first time since I had met the priest, his faith shaken by the secret he carried. He was far away even when attending to the extensive preparation for the expedition, such as finding a ship with a discreet captain and crew.

While those tasks occupied Bishop, responsibility fell to me to keep our provisions in order: clothing and blankets, stakes and canvas to make tents, tools for repairs, oilcloth and steel flints to make fires, stores of biscuits, beef, pork, cod, and cheese, with butter, salt, mustard seed, and assorted spices for flavor, iron pots, frying pans, dishes, and utensils to eat from, maps, compasses and telescopes for navigation, soap, antidotes, balms, and potions for medicinal purposes, and, finally, swords, pistols, muskets, shot, and gunpowder filled the armory.

Our ship was the *Maiden-Made-of-Light*, a small galleon under the command of one-eyed Captain Clint, a jocular sailor and regular ferryman for the Church's missions down river. Alongside me, Bishop, and the ship's crew of twenty were another twenty of the Church militant known as the Shooting Stars. The presence of the yellow soldiers, though aligned with the Sol Creator, made me uneasy, as if the Church aimed to deliver battle rather than a letter. I refused to believe the Hero had fallen so far that he would kill his fellow Yorgosi.

The night before we were to set sail, I was forced to communicate to Bishop that poor storage and rodents had robbed us of a third of our foodstuffs. With a small amount of trepidation, informed by experience with past Bishops, I entered Bishop Antonius' office and found him at his desk, forlorn as ever. "I drown in material concerns when all I wish to do is sit in prayer," he said wearily after I told him.

I was silent, stuck between curiosity and propriety.

Bishop had no patience for such indecision. "Speak your mind, Faron."

"If I may, Bishop," I eyed my superior with, I admit, suspicion. "I have never seen you so ...burdened. The Archbishop handed you a secret scroll. What did it say? How am I supposed to record our travels accurately if I don't have all the facts?"

Bishop shrugged. "So, don't record accurately. Record truthfully. Our Creator gave us five senses for a reason. I want you to use them during our travels."

"My five senses tell me you don't like this mission."

He chuckled. "In that, you are correct. The Church's material concerns are antithetical to our Creator's spiritual quest. Unfortunately, such suffocating 'administration' comes with my office and title. So does 'errand boy' and 'scapegoat,' it seems."

Bishop said to speak my mind, so I did. "The Archbishop feels threatened by you, Bishop. He's given you an impossible assignment because he wants you to fail."

Far from perturbed, he was impressed. "You're quite wise for a page."

I looked down and shuffled my feet. Nobody had ever complimented me like that before. "You'll be a great Archbishop."

Bishop's expression fell. "I don't know if I'll accept."

"What? Why?" I didn't expect that response. The Bishop I knew was pious and dutiful but also fiery and ambitious. He believed in the Church with a fervor I envied. Deep down, I knew his melancholy had to do with the secret scroll the Archbishop handed him.

"Faron, ignorance is humanity's natural state. You must learn to enjoy what the Creator has given you, not fret about what He has not. In fact, I should be questioning you, not the other way around. Before the Archbishop dismissed you out of turn, you were going to speak on the pagan legend Lord Hathur has taken to. This Pale King. I have not heard tell before."

My hairs always stood up when asked to talk about my home. "Well, the legend comes from the pagans who originally inhabited the south, the Zarak, and is supposedly their interpretation of the first meeting with the Church. The Zarak lived without lords or kings, practiced arcane arts, and worshipped many gods, not just the Creator. Gods of nature, gods of attribute and the like. According to them, the Pale King was the first Yorgosi leader they met. The Church records speak of no such figure and instead tell tales of many missionaries sharing the divine Light of the Sol Creator with the natives. But the Zarak claim the Pale King pretended to embrace their pagan beliefs, only to turn on Yorgosi and Zarak alike, claiming godhood and vowing to violate of the natural order." I remember having to stop to wet my dry throat.

"And did he? Violate the natural order?"

"The legend doesn't say, but," I shrugged, "the world is still here."

"The Zarak aren't," Bishop remarked evenly, giving away no overt reaction to my nervous disposition, much to my relief. "Do your parents remain in Hathur?"

My heartbeat quickened. "My father raised me but... well, he died. Didn't have anyone until the Church adopted me. Saved my life, really. I never knew my mother."

Bishop inclined his head. "Apologies, Faron. My own ignorance reveals itself. We have more in common than I knew."

Unsure what he meant by that, I took the opportunity to change the subject. "The Hero was a saint of the Church. He made me proud to call Hathur home." Anger twisted my tongue. "Now he's turned against the Creator and bankrupted the land, all to put on a *play*."

Bishop nodded sympathetically. "I once witnessed a nobleman bet his entire family's estate on his brother's victory in a duel—only to watch said brother lose his head. Do not underestimate the folly of highborn. No, my curiosity lies in Lord Hathur's purpose behind the play. The Archbishop claims '*The Mystery of the Pale King*' threatens the Church's supremacy in Yorgos. Are threats what the Hero hopes to achieve by paying for such elaborate theatrics? Does he seek converts? To spur an uprising? Has he simply gone mad?" He sighed. "Whatever the truth, we shall soon find out."

The journey to Hathur made Bishop's words into a cruel joke, for what was meant to be a journey of a fortnight transformed into more than a moon of disasters.

The mouth of the Queen's River crawled with cogs and barges heavy with trade and slowed our initial entry, but once we passed the harbor, the waters opened to us, quiet and still, a mirage of tranquility. First were the ghost towns. The blackened fields full of dead crops. The corpses floating in the river like so much flotsam. Children whose skin stretched across their skeletons, every bone visible. The clerics who remained spoke of empty chapels and dwindling congregations, warned bandits no longer spared Church missions and pleaded for aid from the Holy City, but Bishop had naught to offer.

The sights, sounds, and smells of rot and decay shook me to the core. Outside the Holy City, Yorgos was *dying*.

For that matter, so were we.

The first death occurred the very first night on the river when a crewman named Slattery took a drunken tumble over the portside railing and into the waters, never to emerge. My heart nearly came out of my chest, and I ignored Bishop's protestations in my rush to the deck—only to find the Stars and the rest of the crew *laughing*. Laughing at Slattery's fatal misfortune, a man with whom they shared meals, space, and conversation, a man who drowned moments before.

My shock must have shown, because the largest among the Stars directed some of the mirth at me. "You look like you gon' be sick, boy.

If only you knew what Slattery done, you'd be spittin' in the river. Never shut his mouth neither."

"All the Sol Creator's children are sacred," I replied, my fervor still fierce then.

The Star did not like my confrontational tone. "The Creator has enough children, boy. He can afford to lose some." He took a step toward me. "Like you."

Bishop made me jump when he made his stealthy presence known by putting his hand on my shoulder, not understanding at the time that he was saving me. "Forgive my page, Lan. He is zealous in his duties. Of course, the loss of any of the Creator's children is a tragedy. We all must cope in different ways."

I have no easy answer for why Slattery's accidental death shook me, or why I believed it a bad portent for the journey. In reflection, I can only say the callousness in the face of death unnerved me. Bishop said such gallows humor was common on the river and insisted I overreacted. There is truth to what he said—but I still couldn't reconcile the loving Creator I believed in with what happened to Slattery and the reaction to his sudden and embarrassing death. The man would have no grave, no tombstone, no legacy at all beyond the echoing laughter of those who knew him best.

I stuffed my disgust away, as was my duty as page, a duty to never be seen, never be heard, to hide my indignation beneath a subservient and unthreatening mask, to paper over my outrage and desires. Such was my duty to the Sol Creator who made me and His Church that saved me. Or so I insisted to myself.

Soon after Slattery, the raids began—woken in the night to the smoky snaps of musket fire and the whistling of arrows in the air. Surprised during the day by wild men with axes who swung on vines to board. The further we traveled, the worse the conditions became, as if the river took us into the land's barbaric past. I ran and hid below deck, repenting to the Creator my earlier discomfort at the Shooting Stars' presence, without whom our mission would have surely ended on the river. The attrition and suffering made me long for home in a way I hadn't since I joined the Church. I prayed to the Creator every night to permit my return home.

Heavy rains and fog followed, so thick I could not see the end of the ship, let alone further downriver. Despite Captain Clint's assurance of his navigational prowess, *Maiden-Made-of-Light* crashed into an enormous oak hidden beneath the swollen currents. The many-limbed behemoth pierced the hull in three places and left the lowest decks flooded. Bishop ordered those of us remaining to salvage what we could and to use the ship's four boats to reach our destination.

Captain Clint, distraught at the damage to his ship, did not approve. The boats were his, he said, and he would not condemn his remaining crew to our "Creator-cursed task."

"You defy the will of the Creator?" Bishop asked sharply.

"I defy the will of a bunch of ponces in robes who think they're better than me," Clint growled. "I served the Church my whole life, and for what? Ain't got nothin' back but death."

"We serve a greater purpose than ourselves, captain," Bishop reminded him.

"And what purpose did the deaths of my men serve? Or yours?" He turned to the surviving members of the Shooting Stars. "Your Bishop hasn't told us the real reason we're headed to Hathur. Are you lot so brainwashed you'll die for a liar over the Hero?"

"You go too far!" I noticed Bishop's telling twitch of the eye when he was distressed.

The leader of the Shooting Stars had his skull split in two during the raid of the swinging axe-men. In his place, the surviving Stars looked to their largest and most intimidating member, the cold, steely Lan. The man's stare alone chilled the blood in my veins. I was sure Lan would join the captain in dissent. In the end, what he did was worse: he defended Bishop and me.

"We serve the Church, not your fucking ship," he barked.

Lan's support proved decisive. The nine other Stars aligned behind him, as Clint's remaining crew of eleven did behind him. Thanks to Bishop, an agreement was reached and violence averted. He would lead the Stars on foot with as many supplies as they could carry while Clint and his crew would remain behind, patch the hull, and return to the Holy City.

Only once we traveled down the forest road and made camp far from the shipwreck did Lan confront Bishop over their mission.

"I saved your ass back there." The hulking Star pointed a finger at Bishop. "What did he mean about choosing you over the Hero?"

Bishop chewed and swallowed a spoonful of the bland stew that was their supper before answering. "The Archbishop believed secrecy was vital to the success of our mission. But I shall not lie to you now: we journey to Hathur to repossess the province for the Church and, if need be, arrest Lord Hathur. His reckless spending has impoverished his lands and robbed his children of their inheritance. We are here to put an end to his financial folly."

Lan's tone changed. "We're here ... because the Hero owes the Church coin?"

The hairs on the back of my neck stood up. A primal part of me knew that tone, that quiet, simmering, threatening fury, and for a moment I was a child again, at my father's mercy. I looked to Bishop, who also recognized Lan's demeanor for what it was. "Our rewards shall be substantial," he added, addressing the company now. "Coin, titles—even land, I'm told."

His promises seemed to placate the Shooting Stars, at least for the moment. Mutiny (barely) averted, our company drifted off to fitful slumber.

The next morning, we woke to discover three of our number missing.

"Deserters!" Lan exclaimed, prowling the camp in his knickers, cutlass in hand. "Cowards!"

My bleary eyes caught up with my rushing legs, and I found myself out of my bedroll, panicked and panting. Bishop calmed Lan and the other Stars while I slowed my breathing. Then I noticed the missing men's bedrolls remained, as did their packs, clothes, and weapons. I gestured at the abandoned equipment. "Bishop? Bishop!"

Lan continued to rage, but Bishop finally turned and saw what I did. He pointed for Lan's benefit as well. "Think, Lan! Would they have deserted without their supplies?" He appealed to the six dumbfounded Stars who were left. "Who held watch? Did either of you witness anything during the night?"

A young Star with a scar under his left eye shook his head in terror. "The sky went dark as pitch, no stars at all, and I saw a *city floating in the heavens*. Tell the Bishop, Amell, tell him."

After a cautious pause, the older, grey-haired Star named Amell spoke in a shaky voice. "I didn't see no city in the sky. I heard a woman scream, as if the trees wailed. I went looking but I – I think I was sleepwalking."

The pair had nothing else to offer, to our disappointment. We spent the morning combing the woods for any trace of our three missing Stars but found nothing, not even tracks. In the end, Bishop gave in first and counseled Lan that, if alive, they would likely seek to reunite at Hathur. It was a poor lie, but one the giant leader of the Stars needed, it seemed, to justify abandoning the search and continuing the mission.

"Three more days and we'll have soft beds and hot meals at Castle Hathur," Bishop promised.

Three days became thirteen.

Those were the hardest days. The will had been wrung out of me. I twitched and jerked from lack of sleep. My clothes were ragged remnants of their previous condition, and my stomach rumbled before and after we ate our meager rations. Lips cracked, mouth dry, tongue heavy as an anvil in my mouth. Legs soft and wobbly, back bent and crooked, feet sore and blistered. Life-and-death stakes just to relieve myself, constantly on guard for on-lookers.

One day, I returned and my heart nearly stopped. Lan stood, staring at the sunrise, his normally vibrant face vacant. "We should have been there by now. Why aren't we there?"

I could only stare dumbly as he wandered away.

Two more Stars died before we reached Hathur. One broke his ankle and suffered a terrible infection that required amputation, only to die after the procedure was complete. The other, the young man with the scar under his left eye, killed himself with a single pistol shot to the head.

Within the gilded walls of the Holy City, suffering was abstract, a topic of discussion; man's decay kept at a distance, the consequences theoretical. I escaped the worst of poverty when the Church adopted me, but even my briefest time as a homeless orphan left me both reverent for and at odds with a cloistered life of comfort. *Be grateful the Church saved you from an early death*, I would think when I felt particularly stifled or trapped.

Ironic then that this Church mission was worse than anything I endured in the gutter of Hathur—at least, until my return.

Part II

The Arrival

*D*eparting with the promise of swift resolution, his later apostasy puts Bishop Antonius' poor performance, initially taken as incompetence, in a malevolent light. Much like Cleric Paulus before him, the Church received no further communication after the expedition arrived ...

-From the official records of the Sol Church, dictated by Archbishop Claudius

---

More than a moon had passed since we departed the Holy City. Of the two-score Shooting Stars who set out with Bishop and me, only Lan and four other ragged, weary souls arrived with us at our destination.

As we stumbled up the road, I first noticed the slow-but-gradual disappearance of trees. Soon, the forest around us was nothing more than a barren field of stumps. Then the sunset broke through grey clouds to illuminate the massive monolith that was Castle Hathur and the town that encircled it. Built of oversized blocks of black basalt, the stone walls rose fifty feet, its towers sixty, and its keep an enormous eighty. From such a height, the lord of the castle could observe his fief from the Queen's River in the east to the smoking mountains in the west, whence came stories of the legendary fallen star once worshipped by the Seven Solara.

Surrounded by death for more than a moon, I couldn't help but laugh with relief at signs of life. *The worst trials are behind us*, I thought. *We are under the Hero's protection now.*

Then I remembered we'd come precisely to take that protection away.

I was about to tear my eyes away when I noticed something through the battlements of the castle keep. No, some*one*. Vaguely human-shaped but blurry and distorted, and not just from distance. The more I squinted the less detail I could make out, as if the face I looked at were a white featureless oval. I blinked, and the frightening figure was gone. *You're not a child any longer, Faron. Put aside your stories. You're on real Church business.*

Hathur had always been strange, even when I was a child. Frontier freedom had lured my father there, a place where he could exceed his station and own land. But peasants stay peasants, else they join the Church, and my father did not like priests. Nor, he discovered, did he enjoy Hathur. Motherless by my birth, I was the perfect receptacle for his hate, a walking, talking reminder of his disappointed dreams. When I joined the Church, I sought nothing more than escape. The Hathur I'd grown up in was grey and brown, a dank and dingy hovel surrounded by other hovels, the scars of battle still upon the land.

The Hathur I returned to was the same hovel but painted white and trimmed with gold, as if the paint had been all that was wrong with the dilapidated shacks that made up the local stores and residences. Packed and bustling as the rest of Yorgos had been emptied, lit by dozens of mountainous bonfires lined on either side of the road into town where, beyond the threshold, music and merriment made their call. Here men and women alike celebrated and danced in its streets as night descended, the crowds dressed in ostentatious colors and elaborate finery despite clearly being peasants with splotchy skin and rotten teeth. I marveled at the masses. The population must have doubled or tripled since I had left. What's more, everyone was older than I was. Eyes followed our party with great interest, but I couldn't help but feel that many focused on me.

Seemingly endless tables of food lined the main street, a banquet replete with quail and chicken, bowls of black bread, a buttery venison stew full of garlic, onions, and carrots, and platters of fruit pastries, sweet cakes, and pies.

Lan spoke for us all. "We've arrived in paradise."

Our guts seemed to cry out in unison, the aromas mouth-watering.

All else forgotten, Lan and the surviving Stars dropped their muskets and rushed for the food. I joined them, stuffing my face full of the first thing I could grab, a raspberry tart with jelly that exploded with sweetness. *Sugar. Real sugar. This cost a fortune even before the famine.*

Legs of chicken, hunks of bread, and a bowl of stew followed. Quaffing water, I realized someone was missing. I looked back, and sure enough Bishop hovered at the edge of town, refusing to partake of the bounty. Feeling guilty, I returned to him, a second raspberry tart secreted up my sleeve for later.

Bishop frowned at the joviality. "Cleric Paulus went missing after he arrived in Hathur." He nodded at my sleeve, eyebrow raised. "He may have been poisoned."

I considered. "Everyone's partaking. The Hero's not going to poison everyone, is he?"

Bishop rolled his eyes. "The sheer fact that you need to ask that question should tell you." He seemed ready to say more when something behind me had made his jaw drop. A jester pranced toward us, gangly and thin, his frilly white outfit dirty at the edges, a bucket atop his head festooned with cowbells, and face painted in yellow-and-purple motley. His right hand was a burnt husk, as if he'd placed it in a fire. Over the annoying clang of his bells, the fool sang, "All the world's a stage, all the world's a stage, a home for knights and knaves, who's the fool when the hero plays?" He landed in front of us and gave an exaggerated bow.

Bishop blinked repeatedly. "*Paulus*?"

The fool wagged a finger, his many bells ringing. "Twinkletoes."

The truth made my ears rang as if a hammer had hit me upside the head.

"When you stopped sending messages, we assumed the worst," Bishop struggled to say.

The former cleric cocked his head quizzically while, behind him, Lan and the Stars shared in the town's festivities. "Messages?"

"Yes," Bishop insisted. "You're name is Paulus, you're a servant of the Sol Church, of the Creator and all His glory. Don't you remember?"

"Hathur's where I am, Hathur's where I've been," Paulus—or Twinkletoes—smiled broadly. "But I've never left the inside of my head."

Bishop's shock turned to sadness. "Come, Faron. We'll find no help here."

He gave cleric-turned-fool a wide berth and forged a path through the crowded street.

"Madness makes sense of a mad world," Twinkletoes' whimsical voice called after us, "when lies told are lies learned!"

I dropped the tart from my sleeve and stepped on it, my stomach in knots.

The seven of us slipped to the town square, where every Yorgosi town built a star-shaped chapel in honor of the Sol Creator and the Church who represented Him.

But that was not what we found.

The chapel where I had first prayed to the Creator was gone. In its place stood an ugly square of white marble veined black, like a spider's web of cracks across the surface the pale edifice. The new building was triple the size of the previous, not high but so wide as to eclipse the entire marketplace, whereas the previous occupied merely a quarter. Pillars every six feet held up the stone sky and beneath it, the square had been dug out to create an enclosed coliseum. A skylight in the roof let in light on the rows of seats surrounding the curtained stage, atop which stood a fully assembled and gleaming white suit of knight's armor. Encircling the skylight was a mural mimicking the night sky, a specific constellation highlighted in the artists' rendition: nineteen stars united to depict a Yorgosi warrior holding the decapitated head of a witch, who legend said he slew for having snakes for hair.

Hooded men in white robes and white featureless masks stood at every pillar and handed out duplicate masks to those who entered the heretical temple. One tried to hand a mask to Lan, who slapped it out of his hand with a snarl, "Creator curse your pagan heresy!"

"Calm yourself, Lan, they are no threat to us," Bishop said. "Fan out with your men and discover what you can of the Hero's performances from these peasants."

The answer, we found, was nothing. The peasants, dressed in discordantly garish costumes, could not stop praising the greatness of

Lord Hathur's play, but when asked about any details in specific, they deflected or denied our requests and returned to unmitigated adulation of the Hero. Of all the people who claimed to have seen "*The Mystery of the Pale King*," none would or could describe exactly what happened in the lord's play.

After several fruitless efforts to extract information on my own, I searched for Bishop in frustration and found him hiding in the shadow of a pillar, not even having descended into the bowels of the pagan temple. Then I saw he wasn't alone. Curiosity my vice, I crept to the pillar and edged around it until I could overhear the pair's whispered conversation above the din of the crowd. The mysterious voice was a woman's, bitter and wry. "—had you not abandoned Hathur for the Holy City, our gods for your One and Only, and your name for 'Bishop Antonius.'"

"Not that any of the effort saved me in the end. Here I am." Bishop sighed. "I didn't seek you out to refight old battles, Maggy. I'm here because of the evil this temple honors."

I risked a glance around the pillar. A guilty Bishop questioned a beautiful plump woman in a black dress, her bushy brown hair so long the locks reached her knees.

"I gave up long ago wondering the reasons men do what they do," she said pointedly. "Convincing others to save themselves is a fool's errand, *Bishop*."

"Don't call me that, not you," Bishop said, abashed. "You know why I had to leave."

"And look where you ended up." There was no joy in her words.

He looked more tired than I had ever seen him. "Maggy, the Church... the Archbishop gave me a message from King Leo himself. Our mission... the lord's forfeiture is merely a pretense. The king has ordered his death. By my hand."

My memory flashed to the Archbishop's secret scroll and dark spots dotted my vision and my head spun. Bishop was secretly from Hathur? His mission was to assassinate the Hero? Either one of those statements alone would have shaken me. Both left me terrified. The Church's priesthood was expressly forbidden from violence; that was the sacred duty of the Shooting Stars. The Creator I loved and worshipped would never ask that of Bishop, I was sure. But Maggy had said Bishop abandoned Hathur the same as his name. The realization that I knew nothing about the man I served left me groundless, as if I hovered over a void.

To my disbelief, Maggy shrugged indifferently at Bishop's agonizing assignment. "What do you wish me to do? To try and save you? To plead with you once more? Not this time. You should leave, Bishop. For your own good."

"I am not afraid of him," Bishop vowed.

"Then you are a fool! Look around you. His play casts a spell upon all those who see it. His words can reach into a person's mind and control their thoughts, what they believe and what they don't, who they are and who they hate. While carrion crows feast on Yorgos, a poisonous flower blooms in Hathur, fed and watered by the lord of the land."

"Does Lord Hathur provide feasts like this every night?" he asked her after a pause.

"The nights before performances, which are often enough. The town is fit to burst or burn, yet the festivities continue."

Bishop shook his head. "He was always ambitious but never mad. What caused this?"

A commotion in the thicket of bodies within the temple interrupted both the conversation and my eavesdropping. In the thicket of bodies that milled around the temple stage, Lan was in some sort of argument with a short, stooped masked man in white. I ducked out of sight when Bishop rushed past, peeked behind the pillar, and found the shadow empty. Maggy was gone.

Given Lan's volatile disposition, I assumed the worst. When I forced my way through the onlookers to reunite with Bishop, my expectations were exceeded.

Lan had a mask in his hands, the towering man's gaze transfixed on the hooded man whom, to my utter disbelief, had a hand on the taciturn Star's shoulder and was preaching to him. "The Pale King is not a deity always out of reach of his followers. He is as tangible as you or I." He beamed at the shining suit of armor on stage. "Through his works, He becomes us all."

A perturbed Bishop stepped between them. "I am Bishop Antonius, sent on behalf of the Sol Church. This idolatry is an affront to His Church. To whom do I speak?"

The hooded man removed his featureless mask to reveal the face of a kindly old man. "Welcome to the Chapel of the Pale King." He smiled a lipless smile and gave a slight bow, more mocking than deferential. "I am Aleister, Grand Arcanist to Lord Hathur."

"Ah, 'Grand Arcanist.'" Bishop wrinkled his nose. "You claim a pagan position that does not exist in Yorgos, in a spot where you defile the Sol Creator. Do we have you to thank for Lord Hathur's conversion?"

Aleister laughed. "My dear Bishop, as I was just explaining to Lan here, Lord Hathur sought *me* out. Naturally, I was skeptical of nobility, who for so long looked down on us, but I am happy to have been wrong. Lord Hathur truly earns the title of Hero! A warrior-poet, come alive from myth and fable. Look at how he provides for those the Church forgot. Why, he even opened an orphanage to house our kingdom's numerous wayward children. You all arrive in luck, for tomorrow is another of the Hero's glorious performances."

"If they're so glorious," Bishop countered, "you won't mind sharing the content of those performances now."

"Oh, I wouldn't dream of sullying your experience. The lord's play is not something you can describe. His words strip you bare, plunge into the depths of beauty and horror, and pull out all that is strong and worthy." He gave a sensual sigh. "His glory is something to be *felt*."

Bishop narrowed his eyes. "Did Cleric Paulus feel this 'glory?'"

Aleister scrunched his brow in a show of sympathy. "Alas, poor Paulus. He was not content to be a spectator. He ate the fruit of his Creator, as Lord Hathur did, and was born anew. I'm sorry to say, unlike our lord, he was not reborn stronger."

"An injury to a cleric under your care is an injury to the entire Church."

"Both Lord Hathur and I tried to dissuade him, but he would not listen." He looked at Lan, and his lipless smile returned. "The arrogance of the priesthood. Insulated in the Holy City, they never face true consequences. Soldiers like the Hero and you understand."

Lan chuckled before he caught himself, and the Star's eyes flitted nervously between Bishop and Aleister. The hair on the back of my neck stood up, only I was too dense with fear to understand why.

Bishop chose to ignore the Star's impropriety. "The Lord's children appealed to the Holy City directly. Where have you done with them? Have they too suffered Paulus' fate, driven mad and dressed as mummers?"

"Bishop, you wound me! Many here *are* mummers, as the lord's masterpiece includes over six hundred background performers, thirty-thousand lines of verse, and one-hundred-and-fifty speaking parts. The attire is salvaged from previous performances. You might have noticed the bonfires outside town? Lord Hathur burns the outfits and has each garment remade for each performance. The peasants salvage what they can. As for the lord's children..."

Aleister gestured to one of his followers, who stepped forward and removed their mask to reveal a young man with a crown of golden curls and a baby face pantomiming hardened determination. "I present Drusus Hathur, eldest son of Lord Cassius the Hero."

None of us had a reply, each looking in nervous bemusement at the other, Bishop included.

"D-Drusus?" Bishop stuttered. "I don't understand."

Drusus clasped his hands apologetically. "I see you are still concerned. Do not worry for the peasants. All are provided for, of course. Plenty of meals and places to sleep. My father spares no expense. Such amenities are likewise available to you." He looked at me and smirked, "I can see you have already partaken."

I furiously wiped my mouth for any trace of the tarts and said nothing, because he was right. A hot meal and a warm bed, those were all I asked for. Suffering had made me amenable to almost anything. I wanted Bishop to back down, if only for those small comforts. If my spirit had overcome, if I had been more resilient... but I wasn't. I didn't see the trap we were in. Not until it was far too late.

Bishop, recovered from his surprise, did not falter. "You, your older sister, and younger brother sent to the Holy City for help. Where are Livia and Julius? Are they—?"

"Quite well? They are, thank you," Drusus interjected pleasantly and snapped his fingers at a servant. "Fetch Livia, I can tell this Bishop shall not be satisfied at our word alone. My brother Julius is like that too. Stubborn. Irritating. It was he who wrote the letter to the Holy City, falsely attributing his words to my sister and me. When we discovered his malfeasance, he fled like a coward. My father is sick with grief but insists the performances must continue."

Bishop and I shared a glance, and I'm sure we had the same thought: Julius had not fled.

Lan and the Stars, on the other hand, were beside themselves. "For nothing?" Lan was raw with barely contained fury. "All this way—all the lives—for nothing?

"Not for nothing, my good soldier, never nothing," Aleister assured with his lipless smile. "On the contrary, Lord Hathur prepared accommodations in anticipation of your arrival. He told me your coming was of the utmost importance to him."

To my surprise, Lan's angry, searching eyes softened. "He did?"

Bishop put his back to the Grand Arcanist to face Lan, the Stars, and the encircled onlookers within the temple. "Do not listen to him, Lan. Or any of you. He leads you astray from ascendance. In his hands, you would be no more than pigs in a pen. Remember His words: 'He who tempts with ease tempts with evil.' What is just and right is never easy, *should* never be easy, because if virtue were, we could not redeem our fallen bodies in the eyes of our Sol Creator and earn, in return, eternal bliss in heaven. These worldly pleasures pale in comparison to the bounty of our Creator!"

I winced, and sure enough, his appeal to austerity did not sway the Hero's flamboyant followers. If anything, the effort amused Drusus and Aleister.

"Typical Church rhetoric," Aleister said. "Navel-gazing behind the walls of the Holy City, telling our people what to do, what to believe, how to feel—"

Bishop drowned him out with a bellow. "Rather than ration for the kingdom's survival, Lord Hathur sold off his lands. *Your homes.*"

Bishop produced the king's edict. "In the name of King Leo and the Sol Church, he must present himself and relinquish control to me."

A woman's voice, high and pouty, answered, "Relinquish control? You might as well ask us to kill ourselves." Servants parted the crowd for the strut of a waif-thin lady with long golden hair. Each tremulous step held a slight waver, as if she were always on the brink of falling.

"Sister, this is Bishop Antonius. We have our little brother to thank for his arrival." Drusus snatched the edict, read, then looked from Livia to Aleister incredulously.

Unlike her brother, Livia seemed more intrigued than piqued, peeked over his shoulder at the edict, and waved a careless hand. "We'll appeal to the king."

Bishop inclined his head. "He is the one who sent me."

Livia Hathur seemed to notice Bishop for the first time and sauntered over with a squint. "Have we met before? There's something familiar about you."

In my memory, he looked at me before answering. But perhaps nerves alter my recollection, shocked as I was after spying on his enigmatic conversation with Maggy.

"My mother was from Hathur. Antonia, after whom my name honors."

The new information made me blink while Livia observed her cuticles. "Hmmm, my brother and I are quite familiar with maternal loss," she said off-handedly.

"My condolences on the passage of yours, my lady. Such a tragedy to befall your father three times in a row."

"The recent one was old enough to be my sister," she dismissed. "*My* mother was my father's first wife. When I was young, I blamed our different mothers for why I never got on with my brothers. Then I visited other castles and saw how much those families hated each other too, even though most of them came out of one woman."

"Enough of your blabbering." Drusus pushed his sister aside to confront Bishop. I took an instinctive step back from the wrathful noble. "No Antonia of repute has ever lived on our lands in my life."

"She died long before you could know her repute. Or I could, for that matter." Though his tone remained even, I noticed something I had never seen before within normally tranquil Bishop—a fury hot enough that steam might have come out of his ears. "But it is because of her that I know what this temple truly is: a tribute to butchery and savagery. The veneration of transgressions against the Creator and His children, surrounded by the lustful avarice of man. I care not for your obligations or excuses, nor Lord Hathur's, for by your countenance you have allowed his evil to flourish, this Pale King whom Aleister worships and you both follow in the vain hope of winning your father's love and respect!" Bishop caught his words and took a deep breath, eyes boring holes into Drusus and Livia. "Enough games. Bring me to him *at once*."

His words roiled the crowd. Only then did the truth finally coalesce in my mind. Bishop *knew* the whole time, about Hathur, about the Hero's history, about the Pale King. His reasons for coming back were more personal than I ever imagined. Only in reflection can I admit cowardice near overcame me, and I thought of fleeing. Seven of us stood against a sea of the Hero's followers, and Bishop and I were no fighters. But he was never one to moderate his devotion to the Sol Creator, least of all to the heretics he condemned, and, though my faith in him was shaken by the secrets he kept, I could never willingly abandon him. For better or worse.

Livia's nostrils flared, and she spoke to the crowd instead of us. "After everything my father sacrificed, the Church only sends its missionaries here when they wish to take something from us. Why is that, Drusus?"

"Because they are jealous of him. Who he is and what he's become." Then the Hero's eldest son tore the parchment over and over before scattering the pieces at Bishop's feet. "A god greater than your Creator. No, Bishop. You shall meet him when he is ready, not before."

The sheer ecstasy of the crowd in response proved the battle well and truly lost.

Bishop clenched his jaw, and I was sure he would have continued preaching, because his anger was not directed at the people arrayed against him, but at himself for failing to serve the Sol Creator. The One and Only is divine, perfect, infallible. His Light saved all whom it touched. Thus, the failure to enlighten the masses was his and his alone. His obstinacy had already cost us Hathur's comforts of rest and recuperation and risked yet more. I couldn't let him go on.

I transcended my fear of drawing attention to myself—no small feat—and stepped forward to tug on the sleeve of Bishop's robes. He looked down as if jerked awake.

Then he blinked, drew a deep breath, and nodded before he addressed Aleister and the Hathur children. "We shall make camp outside of town. If your lord shall only emerge for his performance, then that is where we shall meet him. Until the morrow."

We turned to leave. Embarrassingly, the crowd refused to part for our exit until an amused Drusus commanded so. For an agonizing moment, Lan and the other Stars hesitated to follow, before doing so with shuffled steps.

Part III

The Mutiny

...with no word and no resolution forthcoming, the king asked the Church to deploy the Shooting Stars to restore order in his kingdom, a request we granted to our great sorrow.

-From the official records of the Sol Church, dictated by Archbishop Claudius

———◆O◆———

Departing Hathur's incongruous festivity was as disheartening as our arrival was joyous. The bonfires continued to rage outside of town, and it was around one such flaming pile of costumes that myself, Bishop, Lan, and the four other Shooting Stars gathered, cold, hungry, and exhausted. Instead of hot food and a soft mattress, we had cold rations and the hard ground.

"I shall take first watch," Bishop announced, a meager gesture to appease the aggrieved Stars. Soon, their snores intermingled with the crackling of the fire. I had no such ease sleeping, rolling over and over in discomfort.

Bishop noticed. "Thank you, Faron. For your intervention in the temple."

I didn't know what to say. The Bishops I served previously would never have done such a thing, too proud or disdainful to understand the fear of a lowly page. "Devotion to the Creator needs no thanks," I stammered as I went to my feet and stood next to him, rubbing my hands in the chill.

"What we've suffered, I think we could all use a little gratitude," he advised then knelt. "Pray with me?"

"Of course, Bishop." I knelt alongside him.

"Sol Creator," he intoned. "Shine your light in our darkest hour, enlighten your servants, and illuminate our path. Cast your lantern of wisdom through us so that we may brighten an ignorant world. To all those who dwell in the dark and worship false idols and prophets, give us the strength to cast the light of the One and Only and overcome the shadow of evil. Amen."

We sat in silence, until I could bear it no longer. "My faith in the Creator has never wavered, Bishop." I struggled to speak my next words. "But we've seen so much death, just so we could deliver a *letter*. Did the Creator make those men, the sailors and Stars, all the starving villagers and petty bandits, just to die? Then to find the Hero's bounty in a time of famine, despite his heresy, and yet we, who represent the might of His Church itself, are powerless to stop him."

"What I fear you have seen during this troubling mission is a window into how the Church, which we both love and serve, has been corrupted. The Seven Solara founded the Sol Church to serve our

Creator, but the Church we belong to believes the Creator serves *us*, and thereby the king. For that, we are merely instruments of their will, which they are driven by hubris to believe is divine."

"What is to be done? When shall the Creator deign to save His Church?"

I cringed at the look of disdain on Bishop's face. "The Creator has *already* saved us," he scolded. "We are not alive to pout and moan while we wait for His intervention. He acts through our deeds, our choices, what we do, and why we do it. He does not wish for us to pray for or prophesy His grace, but to *fight* for it, day in and day out. We must look for His grace in every opportunity, every situation, good or ill, even the most senseless crimes."

His words did not comfort me. Anger overruled my good judgment, and I jabbed at him with the truth. "Even murder?"

Bishop narrowed his eyes, his fury tranquil. "If that be a jape, it is a poor one."

I searched for other ways to dissuade him and concluded only the truth would. "Who is Maggy?"

His blue eyes fluttered in shock and then understanding. "How much did you overhear?"

"That you're from Hathur." I looked up at him, unable to keep the betrayal from my voice. "That the Archbishop and the king sent you to kill the Hero."

His glassy eyes reflected the flickering flames. "That's correct."

All my frustrated anger at the abhorrent task poured out. "But the Creator wouldn't compel you to forsake your vows. No priest can commit violence, let alone murder! You could have refused the Archbishop, would have been right to, but you *accepted*." Saying the words aloud shook loose tears, and I had to choke them back. "I fear we are damned."

"Some of us were born damned." He sighed. "Do you want to know why I was made the youngest Bishop in the Church? It's the same reason that brought me back to a home I barely know yet can never seem to escape." He looked up at the sky. "Lord Hathur is my father."

"Lord Hathur only has three children," I insisted stupidly, ignoring the obvious. Lord Hathur's three children were almost as well-known as he, but there were never known to be more than three. Bishop looked as different from his supposed siblings as one could be, enough to make me miss their sole shared feature: their father's blue eyes.

"'Masters and lords, high or low, muster bastard-born, though none may know,'" he said with a tight smile. "Many knew in my case, however, and I was never free of that rhyme, even when I joined the Church. I thought by serving the Creator I could escape where I came from." He looked around and chuckled. "Funny, that."

Such information was more than I bargained for. The entire mission was for that matter. Much and more made sense—his rapid advancement through the priesthood, the king's request that he "take" control of Hathur from its lord, his agony during his confession to Maggy—because Bishop was a bastard sired by the Hero of Hathur.

"How come I never saw you when I grew up here?"

"I was long gone before you were born, Faron."

I paused for a long time before asking my next question. "What about your mother?"

"As I said, her Yorgosi name was Antonia. I know little of her besides, other than she was of the Zarak you mentioned, a woman with deep roots in the land. She died before I can remember. Lord Hathur took me from my mother's family and raised me for a time in that castle there." He pointed at the ancient fortress beyond the town. "Of his legitimate children, my half-brothers and sister, Drusus and

Livia, I never knew. But Julius sought me out years after I'd left. He was like me, you see, discontented and restless, yes, but no coward. I do not believe he ran."

I swallowed and asked, "But if he didn't flee, where is he?"

I'll never forget the hollowness in his eyes. "I fear to find out."

I was sinking though I sat still, my former veneration of the Hero of Hathur soured to shame. Bishop and I sought sanctuary in the arms of the Creator for the same reason: to escape our fathers. "I... know what it's like to have to hide yourself to survive."

His blue eyes flickered with firelight. I suspect he already knew my secret. When the time comes, you shall, too. "We are all the Creator's children," he told me, "even before our parents claim us. My escape from Hathur was the Church. The priesthood was more than happy to have the Hero's spawn in their midst, no doubt praying for a situation such as this."

Once more, the depths of the water I swam in unnerved me. Leviathans lurked beneath my feet, ever moving, unseen and ready to strike. Deep within, a question echoed as if trapped in a cave. "Do you think the Creator is punishing us?"

"The Creator has no need; what we do to each other is punishment enough." Bishop hardened, his sympathy drained away. "Lord Hathur has gone unpunished too long. At dawn, we shall rally the faithful Creationists to confront his pagan idolatry."

Fear further constricted my full bladder. "I must relieve myself."

"Do not wander far," he warned.

"Relieving" myself was never a relief for me, not in the way it was meant, and that night was no different. I journeyed as far as I could stomach, to the edge of the shadows cast by the fires, still too close for my tastes, squatted behind a tree stump—and froze.

Far away, at the edge of the devastated forest, a milky-white figure ambled out from between the tree trunks, human in shape save for one characteristic: it walked on all fours.

My bladder released. From sound or smell, the lurching thing twisted toward me, its smooth, featureless face grayish white like the full moon. I yanked up my trousers before I was finished, piss running down my leg, and fell backward. When I looked back, the hunched thing had bounded from the tree line at an unnatural gait—right for me.

I scrambled to my feet and ran, heart beating in my throat, ran all the way back to our meager camp. When I arrived, Bishop and the Stars were already on their feet, the latter with muskets in hand, alerted by the creature.

Or so I thought.

I dove to the ground to avoid their fire. "Shoot it, shoot it, shoot it!"

Bishop dragged me to my feet. "What has gotten into you all? There's nothing but mist!"

I whirled around. The faceless, insipid creature was gone. Fog swirled in its absence. Had the beast ever been there? Meanwhile, Lan and the Stars wandered far afield, their guns aimed not at any charging beast, but at the sky. I followed their gaze to their heavens above and found them as utter darkness swirling like a black sea. Starless.

Lan's musket drooped, the Star's eyes wide. "A thousand temples in the sky! A city of 'em! Do you see? It's *beautiful*."

I swore I would not lie to you, reader. As if willed into life by Lan's words, out of the blackness, I too beheld a city in the sky. Did I gaze upon heaven, I wondered? But I saw no beauty in the crumbling temples and desecrated tombs, the detritus of a thousand civilizations, devoid of life, howling and empty, save for milk-white shadows masked in cloud and fog, the residents of an ersatz realm that resembled nothing less than a graveyard.

Bishop looked from me to the dazed Stars and pinched his nose. "There must have been something in the food and drink. You've all been drugged! There's nothing in the sky!"

I clung to my mentor like he was driftwood in a shipwreck. I wanted to believe him, for such sights threatened to shatter the veil between truth and fantasy forever, as if the dead city *needed* me to help will itself into existence.

Then screams dashed the floating cityscape like a rogue brush-stroke, its buildings turned into misty tendrils across the sky, and the stars beyond blinked back into existence like cosmic torches. The screams came from the old Star Amell, who went to his knees, hands over his ears. "Make them stop, make them stop, make them stop!"

"Who are we stopping?" one of his fellow Stars asked.

"The trees!" he cried out. "They're *screaming*! It's all I can hear!"

Lan marched to his howling companion and silenced him with a blow to the head.

Bishop rushed to Amell's side and made sure the old Star was alive before he turned to the intimidating Lan. "You could have killed him."

Lan looked down on Bishop with derision, each breath a huff. "You have five exhausted, underfed soldiers, and your pet page be-sides. Whatever else the Hero's done, he has food and beds. He is Creator-blessed! Yet we sit out here, cold, starving, *haunted*!"

Bishop's expression brokered no compromise. "Creator-blessed? He *rejects* the Creator in favor of this Pale King. These cultists would indoctrinate you into their heresy with worldly delights. The Creator is above such concerns, and his servants must be also."

I winced at his words, Bishop's obliviousness on full display. His devotion was an enormous monument that nonetheless cast a shadow of ignorance across his vision, blinding him to the dissent in front of his eyes. But I chose to say nothing, for it was not my place. It would be easy to say my role constrained me. But I chose my role. I constrained myself. And Bishop paid the price.

The agitated Lan grit his teeth. "You expect us to subsist on faith alone." The intoxicated grumbles from the other three Stars showed his discontent was very much shared.

"I share your frustrations. Naught has gone right for us on this mission. Many are not here who should be. We must press forward for them, so their sacrifices may not be in vain."

"You're not hearing me," Lan growled, and at last his true menace dawned on Bishop. "Countless dead on the path to this shithole province. We're out of rations, freezing in the dark because your pride denied us their hospitality. *You're* the reason we're stuck out here. I bet you had a nice cushy chamber in the Holy City. I would have liked that, to worship where our namesake fell—but I never could. Because the Shooting Stars kill, and any man who kills is a sinner barred from entry to the Holy City. Your Creator asked for our souls, and we gave them to Him, sacrifices to maintain the purity of you *priests*." He raised his musket, the dagger attached to the muzzle hovering far too close to Bishop's chest. "Death is the Stars' reward for serving your Church. But here, in Hathur? Here, the Hero bestows life." His eyes glinted. "You know best of all, don't you, Bishop?"

Bishop's eyes flicked between Lan and the point of the musket blade and back again. "It's not too late, Lan. You can still repent." He edged closer, placed a hand on the barrel, and my hair stood straight up. "The Creator shall forgive you."

The leader of the Stars let his musket drop—then plunged its dagger through Bishop's upper leg.

Bishop screamed. So did I.

Lan withdrew the blade with a squelch and spurt of blood. I seemed to return to my body then, because next I was by Bishop's side, wrapping his gushing wound in the nearest blanket until Lan swung the red musket dagger in my face, inches from my eye, so close I could see the blood drip from the blade.

"Time for choosing, you pretty thing," Lan cooed, a twisted grin on his face that sent shivers down my spine. "Him or us?"

Him, I thought, compelled by a sacred duty I valued as much or more than my life. It took Bishop shoving me away for me to come to my senses. "With you. I'm with you. Sir."

"So, you do have a brain," the giant of a man remarked. "Go on then, pup, keep serving your master. Patch his leg. That's the Hero's blood he's bleeding."

He overheard us, I realized too late. Bishop lay injured and lame because I confronted him about Maggy, because I eavesdropped on their conversation, because my curiosity couldn't be sated. I looked down on hands stained red by his blood.

I raised my head and gasped. Not at Lan or his bloody cock-substitute of a gun, but at what stood *behind* him, at the very edge of the dancing shadows cast by the costume bonfires. On two crooked legs stood the pallid monster from earlier, only it seemed to have suddenly sprouted hair. I had to squint to see the beast was draped in bloody animal pelts.

Lan took pleasure in my fear, unaware his presence had been instantly eclipsed at the sight of the sickly sallow beast behind him. "I think he pissed his pants," he cackled.

When I looked back, the creature had vanished again.

"What are you waiting for?" Lan demanded. "Tend to the Bishop! He's no use to us dead."

Then you shouldn't have stabbed him, I wanted to say but didn't, for Bishop's sake as much as mine. I examined the torn flesh of his upper leg and nearly fainted.

"Faron ..." he said faintly. "Always look ... for His grace."

Bishop's encouragement didn't so much inspire as shame me. Even in the throes of pain, my mentor maintained his devotion. I took a deep breath, nodded, and set about my task.

For what our fortune was worth, the blade went clean through the muscle, leaving a deep but treatable wound that would not cost Bishop his leg, so long as he was afforded care by a proper healer. Lan's ugly leer made me doubt such a scenario. Stitching and wrapping his leg took until dawn, much of the time Bishop spent out cold. When the sun crept above the horizon and its marigold glow bathed our party, Lan and his loyal Stars celebrated as if they had caused its rise.

"The Creator blesses you, Lan!" one of the Stars chortled.

"He respects true power," Lan said confidently.

Both statements baffled me.

Morning awoke Amell as well, who claimed no memory of his terrified behavior the night before. Any hope I had for his loyalty to the Creator died when the old Star's surprise at the turn of events gave way to disdain. "Serves the priest right for stranding us out here like this. I suppose this means our guns need a new patron."

Lan smiled and squinted at the rising sun behind Castle Hathur. "We already found one."

We marched past the smoking piles of ash and cinder into the shadow cast by the castle over the town. Carrying the lame Bishop fell to me, an outcome I anticipated and for which I fashioned a crude crutch from a broken spear. When Lan barked at us to move, I had to slap Bishop awake, shove the creaky wood under his left arm, put the other over my shoulders and hobble alongside him, far behind the five Stars who had been sent to protect us.

"Back to town?" he mumbled in my ear, barely audible.

"Yes," I said. "They're going to present you as a sign of devotion."

His head moved in what could have been a nod or a loll. "Good."

I wondered how much blood Bishop had lost. "No, Bishop, bad. Very bad."

"You can... stay with them. Observe. Find out... what's really going on."

"How am I supposed to—?"

"Pretend... to be one of them... find Maggy... where the Hathur children used to play."

I blinked, briefly thrown by memory. "I can't just let them take you."

The pale and sweaty Bishop looked up, his pain contorted into determination as we reached the town, much emptied from the previous night's festivities. "You must. They'll take me... to him. Lord Hathur. I can still... finish the mission."

"Forget the mission! You'll never survive!" Before I could object further, the familiar jangle of cowbells drew our attention, the Stars included. Twinkletoes danced into view, his puffy white outfit and face of yellow-purple motley splattered brown with mud and dung, landed in front of the party, and for a moment, I swore his gaze lingered on Bishop and me.

"Just as pride eats joy, what the Creator births, the King destroys." The cleric formerly known as Paulus smiled and bowed, as if applause were coming.

"Must you harass all who enter, wretch?" Lan snarled.

Back still bent, he looked up and his smile widened. "Like you I was, like you I am, it takes a fool to understand."

Lan shoved Twinkletoes' bucket down over his head, slammed both sides with his hands, and threw the fool to the ground. "Rhyme again and I'll rip your tongue out."

Whether gripped by sense or injury, I'll never know but Twinkletoes stayed silent. Lan spat on him as he led the Stars passed, but Bishop insisted I set him down and aid his fellow priest and former friend. I did so reluctantly and intended to merely drag the fool to his feet and be done with him.

But when I gripped his arms, he gripped back and instead pulled me close with such surprising vigor I nearly tumbled off to the ground myself. Behind the bucket, I could barely hear his voice, but nonetheless each word remains indelible in my memory. "*Fly, deceiver.* The tree is bare, and the King is hungry. Beware, for the King seeks new fruit. Beware!"

My blood ran cold, but I refused to let the fool faze me, whatever his madness. "I shall not abandon the Creator or my duty to Him as you did."

"I didn't abandon the Creator. The Creator abandoned *me.* I came to Hathur proud and righteous, ready to serve His glory. Then I saw what the Hero had wrought: a performance of such horrific beauty, as if a prophetic arrow pierced my mind. I realized if the Hero of Hathur could do what he does and not only survive but grow *stronger*, so could I." The fool's laughter, muffled by the bucket over his head, rang out then descended into what sounded like weeping. "*So could I*!"

"What happened to you, Paulus? What did you see? What did you do?"

A whistle came from behind, a warning from one of the Stars. I forced myself to wrench my arm away from the fool and returned to Bishop.

"What did he say?" Bishop asked, not so feverish that he couldn't tell I returned upset.

"More nonsense. We must hurry, or Lan might decide he doesn't need me."

Should I have listened to the fool and fled? A part of me wishes I had for the suffering I would be spared. But Bishop would scold me for such an attitude. *Be as grateful for the worst of times, as you are the best and you shall know peace*, he would say. I can't say I agree with him. For some, there are only worst times.

Bishop and I joined the impatient Lan and the Stars at Castle Hathur's imposing gates and the pair of guards stationed there.

"Boy! Bring forth the bastard priest." Lan barked. When I did, he shoved me away, dragged him forward, and presented him to the guards, a big grin plastered on his stupid face. "Tell Lord Hathur I bear a gift."

The first guard's tone implied this was usual. "Lord Hathur is not to be disturbed."

"Then tell whoever handles his affairs. His son, his daughter, the Grand Arcanist."

"They are indisposed," the first guard said.

"Aye, ship came in—" the second guard added until the first guard elbowed him.

Lan's grin faded. "Ship?"

The first guard glared at the second and smacked his lips. "Arrived just before dawn."

"This ship, what was its name?"

"What am I, dockmaster?" He shrugged. "I don't know the name."

The second guard scratched his head. "You told me it was the *Maiden-Made-of-Light*—"

The first guard howled with anger and wrapped his hands around his companion's throat. Lan's grin vanished entirely. He raced off westward for the docks, and the Stars followed. I hid my elation beneath the burden of carrying Bishop in tow. Help had arrived!

Then I laid eyes on the ship herself, a sight that cut deeper than any blade could, my brief hope now salt in my wound. The *Maiden-Made-of-Light* drifted half-sunken, five hundred feet out in the harbor, the weathered sculpture depicting the goddess poking out of the water along with the rest of the bow, as if the ship had collapsed upon arrival. An empty skiff, roped to the wreck, rocked nearby. On shore, a crowd gathered around three familiar figures guarded by the same, white-masked followers from the pagan temple. I had been a fool. There were no saviors coming. Only more ghosts.

When Lan slid to a halt, his stupid grin had returned. "Looks worse off than we left her."

Amell had his hands on his knees, the old man panting from the frenzied sprint to the docks. "But why's it here? Cap'n said was gon' head back to the Holy City."

Lan waved a hand. "He was an idiot. They were doomed the instant we left. Sheep without a shepherd. Wolves got to them, no doubt. Zarak, raiders, pirates, outlaws, and the like." He turned to me. "Boy! Don't think I don't see you whispering to your precious Bishop. Tell me, once he's in the Hero's hands, what are we to do with you?"

Though I hated Lan already, his repeated use of "boy" spurred me like no other sin. With Bishop barely awake or upright, I grit my teeth and forced myself to commit the sin of heresy. "I joined the Church because I had no choice. With each bishop I served, I hated the priesthood more and more. Yorgos starves while they grow fat in the halls of the Holy City. Hathur is different. Here, there is plenty for all and no greater concern than one's own pleasures. The Hero must be blessed, by this Pale King, if not the Creator." I left out the part about how Lord Hathur drowned in debts and the "plenty" was already gone.

Lan's eyes shone bright. "That's a good boy." He laughed and the other Stars joined in. Whether he believed me or not, my supplication pleased him. The idea sickened me.

Spectators gathered at the dock stalls parted at our arrival to reveal Drusus, Livia, and Aleister near the shore, surrounded by masked guards. Before I could react, Lan yanked the delirious Bishop away, his makeshift crutch clattering on the cobblestone, and threw him at their feet.

"A disagreement, I take it?" Aleister asked mildly.

"You might say that," Lan said. "See, we were sent to protect that man on the ground. On *that* shipwreck no less. No reason or purpose given. The Church expects its Stars to shoot when told and nothing more. We have no choice in the matter. Death followed us across Yorgos, just to get here, supposedly because Lord Hathur owes the Church coin. But that's not why at all, is it Bishop?" He kicked him. "This ponce was sent because he was the only one who could get close enough for the Church's real mission: to kill the Hero."

The crowd gasped.

"What makes you think he'd get anywhere near my father?" Drusus retorted.

Lan basked in the moment. "Because you have a bastard brother. The Bishop is his son!"

The revelations sent the crowd into frenzy. Aleister croaked for his white-robed followers to clear the dock, and the Hathur guards did the same while their lieges Drusus and Livia stared slack-jawed at the defiant, injured priest revealed to be their illegitimate sibling.

The Grand Arcanist spoke to Lan in their stead. "It seems we owe you our gratitude. While not unexpected, an assassination attempt is nonetheless a *disappointing* gesture by the Sol Church. There can be no mistaking this for anything but an act of war on his family."

The last word seemed to snap Livia out of her daze, while Drusus leaned down to examine Bishop with the same disbelief as before.

"My father told me last night that war was nigh," she agreed, her rigid jaw and posture returned. "He knew this before all of us. That's why tonight shall be his final performance."

Lan raised an eyebrow. "Final? We just broke our oaths for the Hero's cause."

Livia flashed dazzling white teeth, but her smile did not reach her eyes. "And we are eternally grateful to you for allowing '*The Mystery of the Pale King*' to conclude without any interruptions."

"What of everything we saw last night?" Lan sputtered as the other Stars looked at him angrily. "The festivities, the food, and the women? Shall they continue?"

Her smile faded. "Ah, you did not do what you did out of loyalty. You betrayed the Bishop because you expected a reward. Then I must assume that, in the future, you would betray my father too, if you believed you could gain from it."

Amell stepped in, beet red and flustered. "N-Never, my lady! What Lan meant was, he didn't want no distractions from—from our service."

My satisfaction at Lan's distress cannot be overstated.

Drusus roused himself from the bemused inspection of his new-found half-brother. "Your service starts now. Aleister, fetch the Cauldron of Rebirth and take their oaths."

The old man gave the order for the mysterious artifact to be brought from the temple then hobbled over to me, Lan, and his four fellow Stars. "Kneel."

The Stars looked at each other and then at Lan, waiting to see what he would do first. His eyes flitted from Aleister to the Hathur heirs. Then he puffed out his chest, musket held under his arm. "I didn't desert one kennel master to heel before another. The Hero showed me serving the Church don't mean nothing. Now, I only work for myself, like him. You want my gun? Pay me."

Drusus pinched his nose. "You say our father inspired you?"

Lan nodded proudly. "I follow his example."

Livia smiled again. "So do we."

The gun blast followed like an explosive punctuation. Smoke and fumes tickled my nostrils and stung my eyes. By the time I blinked away tears, all was done. Lan lay dead on his back, a crater where his heart had been.

One of the Hathur guardsmen fired the fatal shot, signaled by their liege lords to put an end to Lan's brief affair with ambition. All this would become clear to me later. In the immediate aftermath, I only shook in terror, neither able to move nor stop shaking, watching the blood trail grow as guardsmen dragged Lan's body away and fed it to the bay.

Aleister cleared his throat. "Where were we? Ah, yes. *Kneel*."

Amell and his three fellow Stars rushed to do so.

Drusus pointed at the *Maiden-Made-of-Light* as if nothing had happened. "Your first task shall be to investigate the derelict. None have disembarked, and our boarding party has not returned." His frown turned into a smile with disquieting speed. "But I'm sure you'll have no issues. It is *your* ship after all."

"Aleister shall attend to you in our absence," Livia said, looking down at Bishop. "Our family has grown suddenly, and we must acquaint ourselves." She snapped her fingers, and Hathur guardsmen picked up Bishop by each arm and dragged him back toward Castle Hathur.

"I thought we were to serve you directly," Amell protested weakly.

Livia had already started to leave. "You are serving me directly! Through Aleister."

"My father's performance begins promptly at dusk," Drusus added as he walked away. "It shall be your last chance to join our heroic cause, so don't dawdle!"

Only once they had vanished did the so-called Grand Arcanist waddle over to me, look me up and down, and spread a lipless smile. "Why you look a child! How old?"

"Th-Thirteen."

His tongue darted out to lick away white film from the corners of his mouth. "The Pale King loves nothing more than youth. Now that your Bishop is gone, you need not associate with these brutes any longer. I would be pleased to extend you an invitation to serve me *personally*."

Whatever Aleister's vague offer entailed, I was certain I did not want to take it—and yet, Bishop's last request was for me to pretend and observe. The Grand Arcanist was at the center of the Hero's cult, exactly whom I needed to keep an eye on. I almost said yes.

If I had, I'm certain I would be dead, and you would not be reading this.

As was his wont, Amell blundered his way into something he did not understand. This time though, the ignorant old soldier's idea of saving face also saved my life. "The boy is our servant," he shouted. "He belongs to us!"

Outrage at Amell snapped me from fear to survival. I nodded as if in agreement and sank to my knees alongside the Stars, a watery plan of escape formulating as I spoke. "I – I shall stay. I wish to know what happened aboard and—and earn my newfound faith."

Disappointment doubled the elderly man's wrinkles. Before he could object further, his cultists yelled for his attention. A pair of pale-masked cultists walked down the hill to the dock as we had earlier, each carrying a side of a pole that bore a smoking iron cauldron, the contents so hot the bottom glowed red. They took knees to honor the Grand Arcanist but did not drop their burden.

Aleister spread his crooked arms, the billowy sleeves of his robe flapping like white wings. Bent and hobbled though he was, on my knees, the elderly man seemed ten feet tall. "The time for doubt is at an end. Your oath, once taken, means there is no going back. You join a storied legacy that extends far beyond Yorgos, and noth-ing—*nothing*—comes before your new god. Afterward, you shall be a part of something greater than you can possibly imagine, a purpose that comes before wives, children, mothers, fathers, *all else*. Is that understood?"

The Stars nodded, and I forced myself to join them.

One of the cauldron-bearers handed Aleister long metal tongs. "Raise your right hand out and open in front of you," he commanded us, and gestured for the bearers to bring the cauldron down the line, one at a time, starting at the end farthest from me. "Within this caul-dron is fire undying. Burning coals taken from deep within the holy mountain of Hathur. Witness the wonder of eternal flame. Attest your devotion—and hold godhood in your hand."

Amell swallowed and peered into the cauldron. "I, uh, I gotta pick one up?"

The Grand Arcanist gave exaggerated nods. "Then you shall repeat after me, calm and collected: 'As this coal burns, so may my soul burn in hell if I betray the will of the Pale King.'"

"Aye," he said weakly. "Only... what is his will?"

"His will is that you serve," Aleister glared. "*Without question.*"

Amell licked his lips, perhaps unfamiliar with a corner he could not slip out of, then finally did as he was bid. His howls filled the morning air. His first attempt ended when he dropped the coal in the middle, requiring that he start the oath over. When he finished the second time, he sped through the words and let the coal fall to the ground when he was through. Aleister explained to him that not only did his diction need work, he had disrespected the coal and to try again. The third time, he spoke in agonizingly measured words, deposited the coal back in the cauldron, and promptly passed out from the pain, his right hand a shriveled lump of black blisters.

Three more times he repeated the ritual, three more horrible mutilations to watch before my turn came to reach into the cauldron and experience scalding "rebirth." I have little to say of my tears and wails, only that I needed to learn to write left-handed to record this account.

"The Pale King welcomes you into his power!" Aleister announced while I lay crying. A part of me cursed Bishop, and I asked the Creator for forgiveness. No matter the agony in my hand, my mentor no doubt faced worse. *I shall not fail him*, I thought, devoted and deluded.

Each of us were given bandages to wrap our wounded hands, the Stars guns returned with fresh shot and powder provided, and hunks of bread and cups of water were distributed. A far step down from the feast available the night before and yet more satisfying. I had no idea until that moment how hungry I was, and before I knew it, only crumbs remained.

After that modest recovery, Aleister and his cultists herded us to small skiff off the dock. As Amell and the three remaining Stars boarded, one of the Grand Arcanist's spidery hands appeared on my shoulder, followed by a whisper that sent a chill down my spine. "Though you are older than I'd like, Hathur, the lord and land both, are much in need of what you offer. If you return, find me at the temple." I could not help but notice he said, "If."

When I boarded, the others shot me suspicious glances, and Amell tossed a paddle at me. "Start rowing."

"It shall be midday soon," Aleister called after we cast off. "Don't forget, our Hero's final performance begins at dusk!"

Naturally, the Stars left the task of piloting the skiff to the shipwreck entirely to me and my one good hand. Other than Amell, the three Stars who remained were Rast, Farden, and Gault. I share their names now out of respect to their memory, though I'm sure they'd contend my accuracy contradictory to that aim.

"What that two-faced priest whisper to you, boy?" Gault rasped in his strangled voice.

"He threatened me for turning him down," I shot back, desperate to conceal my fear of the four aggrieved and wounded men around me.

"He's lying," Rast muttered. "We should throw him over."

"Do you want to row?" Amell shot back. Nobody threw me overboard.

Who knows how much time we lost while the Stars did naught but piss and moan about our predicament. I asked the Creator why he couldn't have allowed the ship to drift just a little farther into harbor. By the time we reached the broken vessel, sweat poured down my brow, my chest heaved, and arms hung from their sockets, and I still had to climb the netting aboard.

I fumbled for balance once my feet met the ship's angled deck; one misstep and I would fall into the half-drowned stern. Red trails grew fatter the further up my eyes traveled, and I gasped when I beheld the bow. Blood was *everywhere*—dried, black, and crusty, baked under the hot sun, and no sign of the bodies that shed it. The Stars clung to the railing with their unwounded left hands, and Amell grunted for me to investigate to the bloody bow first. The damage made it impossible to spot signs of struggle, save the base of the broken mast where lay a tangle of frayed rope.

I showed the men the severed ends. "Someone cut themselves free."

"Whoever it was must have been tied up for a reason," Gault rasped. "Perhaps the rescue party set loose someone they shouldn't have."

Fearful Farden twitched incessantly. "There's no sign of them."

"No sign of *anyone*," Amell muttered. "Who sailed the ship into harbor? Why's it here at all? Clint said he was returnin' to the Holy City, damn the consequences."

"They must be below. Boy!" Rast pointed at the open hatch toward the bow. "You first."

Of course, I thought, but within his threatening delegation, I also saw an opportunity. A chance to untether myself from men Aleister, for all the elderly man's hidden venality, astutely labeled "brutes." Below would be my escape or my death. At the time, I considered both preferable to my circumstances.

Scaling the ship's slant was not easy one-handed, nor was lowering myself to the second deck, as the stairs were smashed. I leapt and crumpled on the floor in a heap next to the ruined stairs. Only close inspection made the truth apparent: the stairs were deliberately dismantled.

"What do you see?" Amell called down.

I wanted to strangle that man. I crawled out of the light, and when my eyes adjusted, I gazed aft where water lapped at the edge of flooded compartments, then fore and blinked. Makeshift walls of refuse and debris concealed a bedroll, illuminated by a solitary smoking candle. My heart skipped several beats. Then a hand shot over my mouth mid-breath, and another around my left wrist, and dragged me further into the darkness, the hot breath of my captor on my shoulder. Panic awakened every nerve in me.

A man's voice in my ear was guttural and full of terror. "When I remove my hand, tell him you don't see anything. Do or say anything else, and I shall kill you."

"Boy!" came the disembodied voice of Amell. "Answer me or get a whippin'!"

I did the only thing I could and told the Stars there was nothing.

"Tell them you're going to keep looking and to stay above where it's safe."

I relayed the message and heard palpable relief when Amell replied, "Be quick about it!"

The anger at being stuck between terrified idiots overwhelmed me. In a desperate bid for freedom, I bit my captor's hand, kicked him in the groin, jammed my burnt right hand into his eye socket—and tore away an eyepatch. I backed away gaping at the one-eyed owner on his knees, hands between his legs.

"Captain Clint?"

The once-jovial sailor was unrecognizable. Raggedy clothes made for a much larger man hung from his emaciated torso and limbs like corpse wrappings, his beard an overgrown tangle of thick black hair. One empty socket and one eye wide and wild stared at me, and he smelled as if he hadn't bathed in weeks.

"What d'ya say, boy?" was Amell's predictable question from above.

Clint shook his head vigorously, a finger pressed against his lips.

My anger didn't recede on its own; it took effort. "Just a rat," I finally said back.

The captain snatched back his eyepatch, waddled into the shadows of his grim alcove, and beckoned for me to join him. I'm sad to say that, at this point my journey, such an action did not cause me to immediately recoil, corrupted as I had become by the madness of Hathur. Instead, I followed. To cut through my thicket of questions, I started with the simplest.

"Why did you tear down the stairs?"

"To stop others coming down. Or me going up. Beware the light. That's where it feeds."

To hear the Creator's light described in demonic terms disturbed me. "Where *what* feeds?"

His one eye contained more fear than I'd ever seen in a man. "*The Pale King.*"

What happened next happened slowly at first, then all at once. Shadows scuffled above our heads, unintelligible words shared by the Stars, a sudden scream cut short by a gurgle followed by the unmistakable rending of flesh. Blood seeped between the planks to drip onto my head. I drew breath to cry out and Clint had the audacity to clamp his hand over my mouth again.

"*They're already dead,*" he hissed in my ear.

All I could do was listen to the screams of terror, growls of hunger, wails of pain, and a shrill buzz like a swarm of insects, all glimpsed beyond the shadows of the Stars hunted by an unnatural *brightness*—pallid, cold, and faintly blue—that moved like no person or beast I'd ever known, leaping then crawling then seemingly both at once. Cracks of musket fire filled the air with smoke and a stinging powdery smell to no effect, the pitiful weapons of men useless against the entity consuming Amell, Farden, Rast, and Gault one by one, the brightness more blinding with each meal, until I could bear to look no more. Yet even with eyes closed and hands over my ears, I still heard within the noise the horrific truth of Clint's words, the unbearable gnashing of teeth, tearing of meat and the crunching of bone interwoven with the dying curses and agonized pleas of men confronted by presence beyond our understanding, perhaps from beyond our stars. By the end of the slaughter, blood poured below deck in thick syrupy strands.

I hated those men for what they did to Bishop, yet the thrill of vengeance was hollow. Does anyone deserve such a terrible end? The Creator asks us to forgive our enemies and so I tried. I mourned for the children they had been, if not the men they became. Perhaps they were like me once, enamored with the Creator and desperate to serve, only to learn His Church no longer served its faithful in return, and sought to correct their mistreatment, real or perceived.

I heard Clint mutter, "It's over," and I shoved the former captain aside with strength I didn't know I had. The rush reached my head, spots dotted my vision, and I braced against the debris wall of the captain's hideaway for support.

When I was ready, I managed to say, "Tell me what happened here." For what it was worth, he did.

While Bishop had led me and the Stars over land to Hathur, Captain Clint and what was left of his crew set about making repairs to the damaged vessel, a minor task, he admitted, because he had lied about the severity of the breach. Patching the ship was no issue. The problems began when they set sail once more.

"We traveled upriver," he said, over and over. "The first time I saw Castle Hathur, I thought my navigator betrayed me, had him thrown in the brig, and sailed the other way. We traveled upriver. Then men started to vanish, all except their blood it seemed. Some animal hunting us, some said. A witch's curse said others. I don't remember how many days until... until we saw the castle again. Hathur. We turned around again. We took watches, though none of us could sleep. We saw things. Black stars. White shadows. A city in the sky, floating monuments, and mausoleums that looked like Castle Hathur. We traveled upriver, and we *still* ended up back here... as if all of Yorgos has shrunk to this province. Some of the men convinced themselves they could appease our tormentor." His eye traveled up to the blood leaking through the boards. "Ah, but light can only reach so far into the dark. That's its weakness. The mutineers sailed into harbor, only for the patching to give way. I seized my chance, cut my way loose, and stayed out of the sun. But the Pale King... he demands sacrifice, endless sacrifice." His eye drifted back to me. "Those men who came with you, they was the Stars we traveled with, ain't they?"

I nodded, dazed and dumbfounded. "The last four of them. They mutinied too."

"Ain't sorry to see traitors go to the grave."

The enormity of his confession washed over me. Within his tale were echoes of my own—of Bishop's folly, the Stars' betrayal, and the spell cast by the Hero and his play. "This demon, beast, whatever it is—why do you call it 'the Pale King?'"

He snorted. "You and your Bishop acted all secretive, but I knew why the Church sent us after the Hero. '*The Mystery of the Pale King*,' ha! Men like me lose our livelihoods or get hanged if we speak against the Church. Knowing Lord Hathur was taking the piss out of priests with his play gave us a good laugh. Well, that's what I thought at first."

He plucked a dirty bottle from the floor, popped the cork, drank, and offered it to me. Whatever it contained, I wanted none of.

He drank again before continuing. "The men started to talk funny. Superstitious about native curses, witch covens, and foreign invasions. Got in their heads that the Creator sent them here not to fight but to *serve* Lord Hathur, that somehow only he could redeem the fallen Church and end the long famine. These had been devout men, mind you, some I'd known for years." He drank again. "Nothing I said mattered. Fools thought to make me their offering. But then, the Pale King didn't kill me. He killed *them*."

All warmth seemed to leave me. "I don't understand."

"Neither did I!" the mad captain cackled joylessly and wiped away a tear. "I shut my eye the whole time. Didn't look. Didn't see. Just felt that all-consuming, suffocating brightness. I only looked when it was dark, when it was safe. All that was left of 'em was greasy stains."

"What god kills its own followers?"

He slapped his knee. "You tell me, you're servin' one!"

"The Sol Creator is nothing like this Pale King."

"They're one and the same, boy. There's no mystery, no secret. Yorgosi believe in kings and the Creator. Yorgos wiped out the Zarak. 'The Pale King' is what the Zarak called Him."

"You belittle my faith but say nothing of what *you* believe in."

"I've been a sailor my whole life. Every day at the rigging, I dreamt of captaining my own ship. Even after the raven snatched my eye, ha! Then I got her. This here lady's been my life." His mirth faded. "Now look at her. Look at me. Don't matter if you fight or surrender, the same's coming for all of us. What do I believe in? Not dying. Fuck everything else."

I wished Bishop was by my side to deliver his words as only he could. "You think I'm blind to the Church's flaws, but I'm not. Bishop knows the Church is corrupt. Too many priests serve the king's men and not the faithful. He said it was our duty not to give in. Our fight against corruption was our service to the Creator, how we earned His grace."

Captain Clint laughed. "Grace ain't the way of man. You think Yorgos was built with grace? Hating, hunting, killing, *that's* the way of man. People gotta *want* to resist the beast inside. Children gotta be taught how. Yorgos ain't never been like that. The men of this land *worship* the beast inside, dressed up in nonsense about a divine Creator. A beast kept fed and quiet so long as the kingdom prospered. Now? The conquests are over. The Zarak are gone. Famine reigns. Where is this grace your dear Bishop speaks of? Isn't it obvious these priests don't care? They *never* cared. Why should you, boy?"

"Call me 'boy' again and I'll finish what the raven started," I said through clenched teeth, too stubborn to admit he had a point and too angry to argue further. The captain raised his hands in mock surrender. I couldn't articulate myself at the time, but if I could go back, I would tell him that the fact they didn't care was precisely my reason to. Some of us do not have the luxury of not caring. I had to return to Hathur. Bishop's fate was in my hands.

I looked back at the broken stairs, noted the lengthening angle of the sun's light through the hatchway as well as the creeping water level of the sunken stern, and steadied my stance on the cramped and angled deck. "I'm going to rescue him, with or without you."

Rather than mock me, he grew startlingly concerned. "You can't. I mean, it's not safe."

I narrowed my eyes. "You may not believe in the Sol Creator, but I do. His light did not harm me before."

"But your life is precious! I—I can't let you throw it away."

The question regarding the captain's story that had eluded me, like a whistle on the wind, suddenly became clear. If Clint had been tied up when his crew died, he would have had no role in the massacre. But if he had *already* cut himself free… then his crew died so he could live. Just like Amell, Gault, Farden, and Rast. Just like he wanted me to do for him.

"My life, my choice," I replied firmly.

He sighed. Then he lunged at me.

I was prepared. Even so, slipping his grasp was a near miss as he tore away a piece of my filthy and tattered yellow robes, his filching enough to make me stumble, fall, and slide down the angled deck slick with blood. Fortunately, my destination was the escape route: the flooded stern. I splashed down in the water headfirst, spun beneath the surface, briefly lost orientation, righted myself, then kicked hard and resurfaced with a gasp.

Just in time to see the captain barrel into my chest.

Emaciated though he was, he still outweighed me two-to-one. I sank beneath his weight, hit my head on the deck, swallowed stagnant water, and saw stars. I surfaced again, retched, and barely had time to catch my breath before the bastard attacked again. One hand shoved my shaved head underwater while the other held my left arm at the wrist. Whether he meant to kill me or merely incapacitate me to be the Pale King's next meal, I was not about to find out. My burnt right hand isn't good for many things, but I used it in this instance to grab the captain's hand on my head, pull his fingers into my mouth, and bite hard—and not just bite, but *grind*. He let go of my other hand to try to pry me off, but it was too late. I clamped my jaw hard as I possibly could, jerked my head, and tore off two of his fingers.

The rush from my next breath nearly caused me to black out, though I could hardly do such a thing with Captain Clint howling in pain, a servant of the Pale King in all but name. I made my next breaths count then *dove*.

The swim was the longest of my life, and only by sheer luck did I navigate my way out. I remembered inspecting the damage with Bishop when the tree trunk had first pierced in the hull in what felt like a different lifetime. I knew if I followed each hatchway to the lower decks, I would reach the breach that had doomed the vessel. But there is a vast difference between "knowing" and "doing," and in the deep dark of the flooded ship, with naught to guide me but one functioning hand and the thinnest of hopes, I expected to die. No, I didn't just expect to die. I *embraced* death.

When a shimmering ray of light appeared through a small, jagged hole ahead, I swam as hard as my fading strength allowed and had to wriggle through an opening barely large enough for me, certain every moment was my last. I don't entirely recall my ascent, only my exhausted emergence into the light and the high-pitched screech of my inhale. I had to calm my panicked breaths before I could paddle my way to the nearest skiff. My weakened arms couldn't pull me up, so I swung a leg over first and then tumbled aboard, my whole body going limp after the excruciating exertion.

I bathed in warm sunlight and waited for death to take me until I was inevitably disappointed. I did not feel blessed for my survival. My father had made me thank him for the beatings he gave me. So much effort, so much pain, just to continue breathing, and for what? To suffer further for my sin of living? An idea floated in my head I had never considered, would never have considered were it not for my doubt, my fear, my weakness: the idea to flee. To steal the skiff and simply return upriver. Discover the truth of the captain's mad tales for myself. Either I would end up back here anyway—or I might escape. *Any* chance to escape was better than no chance, wasn't it?

My reckless affair with death from beneath the waves haunted me above. Death's impulse beget selfish, destructive thoughts beget ill choices and worse consequences. *Accepting death doesn't mean inviting it*, I imagined Bishop would say and forced myself to sit up, ignoring my many aches. That's when I noticed the other skiff was missing.

Clint? One of the Stars? As with my inevitable survival, there are some facts I cannot deny to you, dear reader. So, rather than the fragmentary way I was forced to endure the horrors of Hathur, I shall in this case make an exception, specifically to remind you to always see a body before declaring someone dead (and even then, I've learned to be circumspect), as the thief was the sole survivor of the Shooting Stars, Amell.

At time, I was overwrought. Any survivor would doom my rescue effort before it began. Funny that such calamitous distress inspires bittersweet recollection now. The present as it occurs is random, chaotic, unknown. We fumble in the dark, let fear dominate us. Only when seen backward can we make sense of even a sliver of creation. So, we gaze into the abyss ahead in search of our beginning and thus our end. Beginning and end, human and god... rigid constructs inherited to aid our mutual understanding becoming like bars in a prison cell, to deny the frightening truth. There is no beginning or end. We are all perpetually in middle, the middle of chaos that could erase us from existence without reason or malice. I am no longer frightened by what lurks in the dark between the seeds of Sol. I fear the light that shines there.

No alarm sounded when I rowed back to harbor. No crowds gathered, no guards shouted. I would later learn they were drawn off by Amell's return. Such an opening only served to heighten my suspicions, and when I was in the shadow of a nearby ship, I dove off the skiff and swam the rest of the way. I emerged, barefoot and dripping, in filthy yellow rags that had once been my honor to wear. *Find Maggy*, Bishop had told me, *where Hathur children used to play.*

The graveyard.

When I was young, I wanted nothing more than to join my peers where they would dance between the tombstones in the moonlight and spook the littlest children by pretending to be vengeful ghosts. I never went there, not even after my father died, the man who kept me locked up so I wouldn't shame him by stepping outside. Why did I want to go join them anyway? Other kids called me a "freak" and threw rocks at me. Sometimes though, I dreamt they didn't. In those dreams, I was welcomed, appreciated, recognized. I didn't have to hide, didn't have to be afraid. I was free.

Then I would wake up.

Part IV

The Truth

...but unlike Paulus, Antonius' familial connection as the bastard offspring of Lord Hathur means we can say beyond a shadow of a doubt that he was a traitor from the start, an exemplary liar whose faithful fervor was a mask for dark intentions. There is no other explanation.

-From the official records of the Sol Church, dictated by Archbishop Claudius

———◦———

I ducked into an alley and smothered my robes' remaining patches of color with mud. The town's white walls presented a challenging contrast, but the early evening hour cast plenty of shadows for me to dart between on my way to southeast quarter of town. Downhill of and entirely within the looming shadow cast by Castle Hathur sprouted slum houses, seedy dens, and ramshackle stores, the homes of those unable to live elsewhere. My home.

My movement was lost in the town's anticipation of the night's performance. Now that word had spread it would be Lord Hathur's last, eagerness mixed with melancholy. The end of the spectacle meant the end of plenty, that the famine had reached Hathur. There was tension among the believers, between the fanatical and the convenient. Beneath the shouts of the latter looting and scavenging as much as they could, the former whispered in reverent tones of what was to come. Would the Hero dare to crown himself king? Such a declaration would plunge Yorgos into open war, a notion that seemed unfathomable to me. I would have thought the same of others in town, as my youth in Hathur had been full of praise for King Leo and the vigorous defense of Yorgos. But the prospect of violence seemed to excite rather than frighten those around me. To see and hear many of the same agitators now condemn the kingdom to war with gusto turned my stomach. *The Hero did this*, I thought. *He poisoned their souls with heresy and despair.* But I had it backward. I realize now what I didn't, couldn't then. What poison the Hero peddled could only take root in a sickly land, its people suffering a prolonged and fatal ailment. A people who embraced death and never let go.

Burial on high ground was an unaffordable luxury where I grew up. Our graveyard sat along the edge of the river and regularly flooded in the spring. Afterward, it wasn't uncommon for remains to wash up, fat and bloated. Children used to play a game to see who would get closest to a corpse. When I passed under the rickety wooden archway that read HONURED DEAD in crooked hand-scrawled letters, I slowed to a stop. The number of wooden stakes and tombstones had grown substantially since I had left, and several spots showed signs of previous tenements that had been knocked down to make room on the crowded riverbank. Smoke puffed from the chimney of a dim hut at the opposite end of the graveyard, braced against a tall conical slab of black rock strikingly similar to the kind that made up Castle Hathur.

Rather than crossing to the hut, I looked around the area closer to the entry, searching for something I had never seen before. The grave I sought would have no tombstone, and the marker –— if one even remained—would be weathered and perhaps unnamed. None of that mattered. I *had* to look, even if it was a fruitless endeavor. A part of me hoped it was.

I found him moments later.

No tombstone marked my father's grave, but rather a plank that read MARCUS, BELOVED HUSBAND, FATHER, BLACK-SMITH, was nailed to a chipped and waterlogged stake.

My heart weighed a hundred stone. How long before I spoke, I have no idea.

"I used to pray for your death every single night. By the Creator, did I *hate* you. I hated that you were a *part* of me, like a stain I could never remove. You made me wish I was never born. But when I prayed to the Sol Creator, I could imagine a different father, one who wasn't ashamed or scared of his child, who loved and, and, and cared and *protected*. When you were gone, for the first time in my life, I was free. And what did I do with my freedom? I joined the Church—and ended up right back here with you." I scrunched my eyes to staunch the tears that welled.

A familiar woman's voice spoke soothingly, "Ghosts live within us, child. We cannot escape them, no matter how far we run."

I leapt in fright. Without my notice, Maggy had sidled next to me in the same black dress as the day before, her long brown hair braided, and hands folded over her belly.

I had to take several breaths to calm myself. "How long were you standing there?"

"Long enough." Her dark eyes observed my burnt hand. "You're Bishop's page, yes?"

"You have to help," I sputtered without thinking. "They took him, they're going to—"

"Not here." She beckoned. "Come with me."

She took me to the darkened hut. The stone beside it was larger than I expected and engraved with a script I did not know. The symbols were short and stacked, like lists. Maggy removed a lantern that hung next to the door, lit it, and entered. The hut was one room sparsely furnished save a cot, a small Sol shrine in the corner, and a fireplace full of smoke but no fire.

Maggy opened a hidden door built into the fireplace and disappeared, save for the faint glow of her lantern. I stood still and blinked away sweat until she craned her neck back out to look at me expectantly. I took her cue and followed. Adjacent to the fireplace was an earthen stairway into the ground. When I crossed the threshold, she closed the hidden door behind us.

My breath appeared the deeper we descended. I thought about the bodies buried behind the walls of dirt and I rubbed my arms. "How did you hide something this big?"

"Your people tolerated my presence so long as I tend to the graveyard. Their ignorance is to our benefit."

It seemed an eternity before the stairs terminated in another door, this one conventional. She knocked and spoke through the crack to an unseen gatekeeper before the door opened fully. Beyond, fires crackled, and people whispered. I passed the gatekeeper, an imposing man, dark haired and eyed like Maggy, with tentative steps, and looked up in awe.

A canopy of tangled black stone roots, some as large as tree trunks, others as thin as reeds, twisted from the ceiling a hundred feet above our heads like gnarled fingers. Paths had been fashioned between the pillars of rock, each carved with similar symbols to those on the rock above. That was when I realized it was all one stone. The black rock above us was no ordinary rock but a *petrified tree*. I had never seen anything like that cavern or the tree that created it. Nothing like it was supposed to be possible. Not in the Yorgos I clung to.

Maggy stopped so suddenly, I almost ran into her. The center of the cavern had been cleared to accommodate a firepit surrounded by dozens of tents. She approached one of the tents, and without a word the occupants offered us food: corn, nuts, seeds, apples, berries, and peaches, and more I couldn't identify. My stomach rumbled but I refused to partake—that is, until two children, a boy and a girl, both younger than me, joined in the bounty. The boy poked the girl, pointed at me, and giggled. The girl hid her shy gaze but waved for me to join. Once I started eating, my stomach took control, and I shoveled bite after bite into my mouth, washed down with enough water to wet my whole face. The boy giggled again, and this time the girl did too.

Six singers around the firepit drew my attention, each wearing white face paint and red lips. One by one, each reached into the flames and withdrew a smoking stone. None flinched or seemed in pain at all. They started to ululate in unison and chase around those in the crowd in some sort of dance. Over and over, each would proffer their stone to another unless they performed some ridiculous task such as standing on their heads, running in circles, even stripping naked. Others gave offerings of blankets, beads, tools, staffs, carvings, and other assorted heirlooms, while others still merely pointed fingers and laughed in apparent mockery. The children loved it.

"Are Zarak priests mad?" I asked with an edge of fear at the sudden chaos.

Her nose wrinkled. "Do not use those words here. 'Zarak' is *your* word. Within your single word are countless different communities secreted away, within Hathur and beyond. Yorgosi subsume and dominate rather than learn and share in humility because Yorgosi instinct is *fear*. Those you call 'mad' remind us those who claim power over others are just that: fools."

I nodded, even though I didn't entirely understand at the time. "There are other caves?"

"Of course. The same root systems extend for miles and connect to other caverns created by our Mothertrees, some used as reverently as ours, others simply for communication."

"That's glorious!" I exclaimed. "You can ask them to help us save Bishop."

She took me by the arm, led me away from the others, and when we were far enough, she set the lantern down. "There is no 'us.'"

My elation died. "Why not?"

"Because I'm leaving."

"Leaving? What about Bishop? You scolded him for leaving and now you are? They're going to *kill* him."

"Such is the risk of an assassin."

"That's not fair! He does the will of the Creator."

"Is it your Creator who forces a son to kill his father or your king? Your Bishop came here to be Lord Hathur's executioner. No different than a royal headsman."

She was right, of course. Bishop knew well the compromises he was making. I, however, refused to admit such, because I didn't want to admit that the man I looked up to had failed. Somehow, out of all the smashed beliefs and dashed hopes, that hurt worst of all. Some truths are too painful to accept all at once.

I started to hyperventilate. "The Creator is all-knowing, all-powerful. He—He could stop this madness any time... Why doesn't He stop this?!" Maggy guided me away from the others and helped slow my breathing. I sobbed into my hands, never more lost in my life.

She sat next to me. "You want to know why I'm leaving? Then listen. Lord Hathur's play shall end tonight. But his followers? Their hate shall not stop. I have seen the horrors Yorgosi are capable of, over and over, without change, without end. Those who live alone have no choice save to leave. So, I'm going elsewhere." She cast a hateful gaze up, nostrils flared. "I hate this town, hate to be a 'Zarak' woman here, where my peoples' butchers are praised as heroes."

The cave was blurry until I rubbed my eyes. "I understand."

"You do? That's good. Because I don't understand you. You hide among ignorant men to serve a god who deems your very existence unworthy."

My hands and feet were cold. "I don't know what you're talking about."

"You can hide from priests, sailors, soldiers, and aristocrats, but not from me. Tell me, is Faron you true name – or did you choose it because it can be male or female?"

I had pretended so long, I had forgotten who I was, who I'd always been. I swallowed, each word a struggle. "My mother named me. At least, that's what father said. I barely remember her. Just a feeling. Warm and all around, like a blanket. Then she was gone, and I was alone with him. He hated that I was different, that I wasn't the son he had wanted or a daughter he could be proud of. He told me I couldn't leave his sight because if I went outside I would embarrass him. I couldn't look at him either, because he said I have my mother's eyes, and they reminded him too much. I learned to survive his rules, but the only place that was truly safe was inside my head. Then my father, he died, and for the first time I was free. Only things I was ever good at were hiding and praying to the Sol Creator, so I thought the Church would save me. But I didn't want to be forced into a convent like other girls. I—I wanted to be a priest."

"Disguising yourself for so long couldn't have been easy."

Her understanding released an aching knot in my heart, cradled in the dark of the cave. "No, it wasn't. But in a way, I wasn't disguised. I've always been this way, but because my father kept me hidden, even those in Hathur didn't know what I looked like. All I had to do to join the priesthood was keep my head shaved and make water when none looked, even if I had to hold it the entire day. The first night in the Holy City, one boy accused me, and I bloodied his nose. I spent many days and nights of solitary penance. The rumors didn't stop, but I told myself if I stayed, if I *proved* my devotion to the Church, if I surpassed all expectations, the other Bishops and pages would have no choice but to stop doubting me. Then they would... they would..." I started to sob again and didn't know why.

"Breathe, child. What would they do?"

I hung my head and whispered, "Accept me."

She tipped my chin up, her dark eyes softened by the faint firelight. "You cannot hide who you are forever, Faron. Sooner or later, you *shall* be found out. The question you have to answer is not whether you deserve a place in the Church. It is whether the Church deserves *you*."

I dried my tears. "I have nowhere else to go."

"You can leave with me. You don't owe Bishop or the Church anything."

I wanted to agree. After all I'd been through, how could I not? But I couldn't. The idea of knowingly leaving Bishop behind was like a jagged knife plunged in my heart. "I *can't* go. The Church may be unworthy, but Bishop isn't. He believes Yorgos can be better, *has* to be better, for the Sol Creator has blessed us."

I worried I'd disappointed her, the first person to whom I ever confided my secret. Instead, Maggy seemed amused. "Come with me. I want to show you something."

She picked up her lantern and led me through the crowd of her people. Dark eyes followed me that I did my best to ignore. We passed beneath a canopy of rocky roots on a well-worn path to the opposite side of the room,

I looked closer at the lines of lists carved into the twisted stone pillars. The symbols covered every inch of them. "I saw these symbols above too. Is this your language?"

"We carve the names of our dead into the Mothertree so they might one day be reborn."

When we were distant enough that the firepit became a flicker and the glow of Maggy's lantern was all that kept us from being swept up in darkness, we reached a cavern wall, and she raised the light and illuminated an enormous fresco, colorful, primal, elegant, ten or twelve feet tall, both carved and painted in a style I had never seen before, baffling me for a moment before I understood what I gazed upon. What first looked like a night sky was a dark forest interspersed with shadowy outlines of people sitting cross-legged, hands held high as if they lifted up the sky. She raised her lantern higher and began to walk along the fresco, revealing the scene as she told the story. Above the first scene was a woman with a giant pair of eyes, long, darting tongue, six writhing arms, and a necklace of severed heads.

I didn't want to admit She frightened me. "I–I've never seen pagan artwork before."

She snorted. "Yorgosi call everything they do not understand 'pagan.' To your Church, there is no difference between Lord Hathur's cult and our faith. Those sitting in prayer are the *Imantaji*, 'dwellers-in-darkness,' ones who modeled discipline, resisted temptation, and mastered self. Only those who achieved total peace and balance within could join their ranks. Yorgosi learn to fear and despise the darkness, but we have no fear of She Who Is Many."

In that moment, everything I thought I knew changed. "Your Creator is a goddess?"

"Nothing so simple as a male or female embodiment or personification. You must look beyond the dichotomies forced upon you, Faron. The Church would have you believe there can be only one absolute god, modeled by men like King Leo and Lord Hathur. Our gods would never constrain themselves to one gender or form, particularly one as limited as a human body. Just like the black sea between the stars and the darkness of the watery deep, the Divine Mother is *infinite* possibility. Limitless potential. Before all else, there was She, formless, ever-changing, a rushing river, giving and taking both. Without Her, *nothing* could exist."

Maggy moved her lantern to the right and unveiled the next scene: a milk-white comet streaked through the image of Divine Mother, the smoking mountains created by the impact of this ancient celestial event immediately recognizable as the peaks of Hathur. Over the next several murals, the milk-white comet rose and fell from the mountains like a perverse sunrise and sunset, a cycle interrupted by the arrival of men in white bowing before the shadowy outlines that represented the *Imantaji*.

"Those are Church missionaries," I realized.

"When the first Yorgosi arrived, they met with the *Imantaji* and claimed interest in our laws, our gods. Our leaders were shocked to discover the cruelty with which your people punished the disobedient, the rampant desecration of nature, and disregard for inner peace and balance in favor of material gain. Your missionaries were likewise baffled, as if ideas of freedom and justice had never occurred to them. Yorgos had been blessed by the Sol Creator to be the greatest kingdom on earth, they said." She nodded at me knowingly.

Church missionaries spent their lives converting others. They were reasoned, experienced, cogent, the inarguable arbiters of a holy life. Yet, I had never learned that they came away from their first meeting with "pagans" shaken and afraid. "What did your priests say?"

"*Imantaji* teach everything is one life, not just plants and animals but the air we breathe, the water in the river, and the fire in the mountain. All is Divine Mother. But Yorgosi treat everything as disposable. Stone, earth, animals, even people, their own *people*. Our knowledge was given freely, as was custom, believing that your missionaries were bereft, and they would be honor-bound to gift something in return. My great-grandfather was there, spoke for the sages. He said Yorgos embraced not true freedom, but the chains of absolute power, offering temptation then punishing those who succumbed, based on the belief that all peoples are evil and need correction. 'Your way is a trap,' he told them."

She revealed the final fresco: a pale cloud erupted from a mountain, spreading over Hathur like a wave, and emerging out of the wave at its forefront, a male figure with a white oval for a face and four phallic limbs, dissolving into thousands of dots until I realized the man and the wave were made up entirely of dots as well.

I swallowed. "Is that the Hero?"

She shook her head. "What you call 'the Pale King' was never simply a man, no matter Lord Hathur's pretension that he and it are one and the same."

"Aboard the ship, it came and killed the men with me. Why? What *is* it?"

She was very still, and I realized she was afraid. "The mountains hide an entity of insatiable hunger and malice, forever severed from Divine Mother. We know it only as 'the *deadlights*.' To look upon it is to be driven mad, left empty of morality or feeling, a hopeless husk, a death-seeker. In the end, the deadlights devours itself."

I struggled to act like I wasn't scared too. "Why?"

"Because death is preferable to a life without Divine Mother. What's happening here in Hathur was the inevitable end of Yorgosi dominance. The man you know as Bishop never accepted the truth about the Church he served. The fool thought he could change the priesthood from within. Instead, he became yet another pawn for the king to use and discard." Her voice broke for the first and only time. She took a deep breath and cast the lantern light on me. "Don't fall victim to the same folly."

I wouldn't budge. "Bishop challenged me to seek the Creator's light in the darkest of times. Please understand, who would I be if I didn't at least *try* to save him?"

"Alive." She put her free hand on my shoulder. "Faron, you've seen much since your return. Gluttony, betrayal, murder, and more. What *didn't* you see until now?"

The answer came slowly then all at once. I recalled what Aleister said to me, stranger still in memory. *The Pale King loves nothing more than youth.* The many sights and revelations since arriving in Hathur—the Hero's extravagant festivities, Bishop's confession,

Lan's treachery—had blinded me. I did not see what was in front of me. Or rather, what was missing.

"There are no other children in Hathur."

Maggy held the lantern close to her face so I would not mistake her words. "Your Hero takes them to the castle. Children of wealth are held hostage to force a ransom. But for every one of those, many more simply vanish. When the lord's men came for Yorgosi children, your people did *nothing*. Nothing while their children vanished, never to be seen again, the disappearances doubling every night your Hero regaled them with his perverse spectacle. When Bishop came, I had a glimmer of foolish hope, a hope dashed the moment he spoke. The Church's pet came not because of the children but because of *coin*."

Though she spoke of Bishop, her comment applied just as much to me. Perhaps that was why I plunged forward with such absurd defiance. I refused to be dissuaded from my mission, a mission I believed was bestowed by the Sol Creator Himself—and perhaps Divine Mother Herself too. "I don't want to hear anymore! If you won't help, fine. I'll do it alone!"

I ran away from her, like the foolish child I was. Too much like Bishop, both of us pretenders living in different skins, ashamed of where we came from. But you aren't reading this account for pity, are you, dear reader? No, what you want are answers. You want to know what *exactly* happens in "*The Mystery of the Pale King*." I thought I did too.

Maggy found me beneath a web of stone roots in a darkened corner of the cavern. "If I cannot dissuade you from glare of the light, I shall at least help you out of the dark."

"How?" I sniffed.

"My people explored these caves long before Yorgos forced us to live in them. I can grant you leave, if you wish. Your beloved Bishop, if he yet lives, sits in the castle dungeon. You shall have to free him before the play commences at dusk."

"Why? What's in the Hero—what's in the lord's play that no one talks about?"

"Our buried history as he's written it, with innocent blood."

Terrible thoughts made me stutter. "He wouldn't... no, not... not from the children?"

"He uses vast quantities of blood in his production. We can think of no other source."

All desire to hear more about the play evaporated then. What purpose could require the use of so much blood, *children's* blood? I clutched my stomach to keep from retching and shuffled to catch up to her closer to the firepit. "His people, my people, cheer this?"

"Do not try to understand. Your Hero may have written himself the role of 'Pale King,' but the deadlights defy man's control. He who thinks he is its master is its puppet."

She brought me next to the firepit and announced me to the congregation in a language I did not know. I shrunk when the six who performed the scalding-stone ritual looked at me. Then one of the six, a pregnant woman, said but a few words. Maggy replied with one. Whatever they said, I'll never know for certain, but I think the only reason I was allowed to leave the cave was because of Maggy's words. I wondered if what I felt was what it would've been like to grow up with a mother.

I followed her to where the light of the firepit leaked into the mouth of a narrow tunnel, just far enough for me to make it out in the dark. Maggy handed me her lantern. One-handed, I sagged under its weight, much heavier than she'd made it seem.

"To go forward, always take the left," she directed. "Always left, never right."

The thought of stumbling alone in the tunnel prickled my skin and made my mouth dry. "Won't that lead me in a circle?"

"Do as I say if you wish to see Bishop again. If you take every left, you shall reach a staircase to another of our hideouts above." She grabbed a pendant hanging around her neck and yanked it free. Another black stone carved with what I believe to be Maggy's name in her language. "Give this to our guard. They know what it means and will let you pass. As for Castle Hathur, you need to find a way in yourself. Lastly..." She hesitated before withdrawing three long, leathery leaves and stuffing them and the pendant in my filthy robes. "Chew the oleander if you are caught; otherwise, don't touch them. And Faron? Do *not* let them take you."

I didn't want to go without saying something. How childish. "I'm sorry for what happened here. For what Yorgos has done."

All sympathy vanished from her face and voice. "Pity is another form of hubris. People must be demons or angels? No, Faron. We are you. You are us. Just people. Now go."

She turned her back and left me rooted to the ground. Abandoned though I felt at the time, I've come to think that such terseness was because she could no longer bear to watch me barrel back toward doom. You cannot save people from themselves.

Alone in those dark depths, bare feet scraping against the craggy ground, guided by a dying lantern light that extended to the cold sweat dripping down my nose, my emotional pique subsided, and regret seeped into my thoughts. I struggled to fathom my circumstance: betrayed by the Church and the Hero alike, aided by those I would have dismissed as pagans a day earlier, on an impossible quest to... rescue the man who brought me into this hell? A supposed mentor who lied about who he was and why he was sent to Hathur, never once warning me of the deadly trap we walked into. Maggy was harsh, but so was the truth. The one decent priest I'd known was a liar and would-be assassin. How stupid was I to think the Church would be different than it was. Why didn't I see the truth then? I had been *free,* but I fled right back into chains, repeating the only lessons my father ever taught me: to hide, to please, to scratch and claw for his love, even after he died. Even at that very moment, in that endless tunnel.

Left after left after left, and then left again, my left arm was barely able to lift the lantern, not that it mattered because the dying light barely extended beyond my body. I began to feel dizzy. Any moment, I expected to end up right back where I started, in the cavern of the Mothertree, so much so that I was utterly unprepared when I reached the stairs I sought, tripped, dropped the lantern, and heard glass shatter on the stone floor. I stumbled up an interminable amount of steps until I ran face first into the door. While I wiped blood from my nose, a slot opened in the door and dark eyes looked down on me in distaste. I fumbled in my robes, withdrew Maggy's pendant, heart skipping when my fingers brushed the oleander leaves, and held it in front of the eyes. With a glint of recognition, the slot slammed shut, and the door swung open.

The guard was a man with dark hair even longer than Maggy's. He snatched her pendant from my hand and asked me a question in his native tongue. I could only stare blankly before he rolled his eyes and waved a hand. "Come," he intoned.

I followed him through a cellar to finally reach the surface, an inn operated by the guard and another woman. The same inn we would have stayed in, were it not for Bishop's pride.

The man explained to the woman in their tongue, handed her Maggy's pendant, and returned to the cellar. To my relief, my new host spoke Yorgosi. What she had to say, however, was very much not a relief.

"All of Hathur is looking for you, child," she said on the way through the kitchen. "One of your Stars, Amell, returned from your ship first, ranting and raving about a demon of light that slaughtered his fellow soldiers. He claims you somehow summoned it. Many are convinced you are the humble guise of the Sol Creator Himself, come to earth to smite Lord Hathur, punish heretics, and avenge Hathur's missing children."

I stopped dead in disbelief. All of Hathur, terrorized... by me? "You can't be serious."

She glanced back with a hint of humor. "Are they right?"

"Of course not! I'm just here to free Bishop before—before anything happens to him."

"Your Bishop's already free. He has renounced his faith in the Sol Creator to follow the Pale King. He preaches in the Chapel as Lord Hathur's honored guest for his final performance."

The words hit me like a hammer to the face while mine failed me. The likes of *impossible*, *nightmare*, and *calamity* could only approximate the depth of my devastation. "A trick," I muttered, rubbing my burnt hand. "He's pretending. Putting on a show."

She pursed her lips. "I know not, child. But if you wish to find out, time is short. Dusk approaches, and the Chapel has already begun to fill."

Dusk! I'd spent more time underground than I thought. My mind raced to figure out how to reach the Chapel. "Do you have white robes? And one of their masks?"

I anticipated either a flat "no" or her disapproval, but instead she left and returned with just the disguise I needed and nailed wooden lifts to my shoes for good measure. My host disposed of the ragged remains of my yellow page robes while I changed, beckoned me when the atrium was empty, and pointed out the front window where the sunset yellows and purples comingled on the cobblestone street. "Go south until the street forks. Take the left and you shall reach the Chapel."

I lifted up the suffocating mask, both to steady my breathing and ask her a question. "Why aren't you trying to stop me? Everyone else has."

She withdrew Maggy's stone pendant and dangled it in front of me. "Do you know what this is, child?"

"My name is Faron."

She inclined her head. "Heartstones are our peoples' most precious ancestral heirlooms, Faron. Within them is all the wealth our people ever have or ever need. Whatever you need, I do not question. By giving this, Maggy has paid in full."

Even more than a lack of kings, I struggled to imagine a world without coin, a marketplace of gifts, of the immaterial. Such an idea seemed as impossible as, well, the idea Yorgos would fall. But I wasn't thinking about the future at the time. All was blotted out by heartache. I'd thought Maggy had given up on me for a lost cause, another witless instrument of a kingdom she had every reason to despise, a kingdom I too had grown disillusioned with. Far from sending me into the night with nothing, she had given me her *everything*.

The knowledge weighed heavy on my shoulders. "Can she ever get it back?"

To my surprise, the woman smiled slightly as she pocketed the pendant once more. "Only a Yorgosi would need to ask. Of course. To keep it would be taboo. Heartstones belong with their bloodlines. I shall return Maggy's when we reunite and safeguard it as if my own until then. All in Divine Mother's time."

I thanked her, checked again on the oleander leaves hidden in my white robes without touching them, took a deep breath, slid the faceless mask back on, and slipped out of the inn. I nearly tripped twice before I adjusted to the three-inch lifts haphazardly attached to my shoes. Most were still taller than me but at least I no longer seemed a child, the most dangerous thing to be in Hathur.

More and more people—outfitted same as me, though some had yet to assume their mask—filled the street when I approached the Chapel which, as I feared, was heavily-guarded by Lord Hathur's musket-wielding men. At each entrance, pairs inspected unmasked faces before allowing them inside. Just as I wondered how in the Creator's name I was going to distract them, the bucket-headed answer cartwheeled into view.

"The end is nigh, the end is the nigh, my oh my, tonight my friends, the end is nigh!" Twinkletoes sang while he performed to the cheers and jeers of watchers.

"Someone should shut the fool up for good," a masked man growled.

"Blasphemy! He's been touched by the Pale King!" someone else claimed.

"Aye, he foresaw the Church's treachery," another shouted then asked Twinkletoes, "What else do you foresee?"

Twinkletoes stumbled out of his last cartwheel, adjusted the bucket on his head, and raised his hands high. "Hathur's light shines bright, whether day or night. Bask in the glory the Hero bestows, the fruit of knowledge he has grown. The only earthly truths are power and pain; all acts permitted, all taboos broken, all as the Hero says! Worship the might of his song and forget the difference between 'right' and 'wrong...' 'good' and 'evil...'"

His blank gaze wandered until his eyes landed on me, and suddenly they did not move. Neither did I. The crowd roared unanimous approval, and none seemed to recognize he'd stopped rhyming. His hands dropped and he blinked, as if he'd forgotten where he was. Did the part of Cleric Paulus that lurked behind the yellow-and-purple motley face recognize me then, even disguised? Or was what he did next simply madness?

He bounced his way to a pair of Chapel guards and snatched away the nearest man's musket. The guard cursed, "Put it down, you bastard!" and shouted at his indecisive partner, who pointed his gun half-heartedly, unsure of how to react.

Twinkletoes swung the weapon around in a wide circle, scattering the crowd and keeping its owner away. "The cost must be paid, the bill has come due! The time comes to embrace our doom! *Forgive me, my Creator*!" Then he aimed at the indecisive guard, there was a crack, a puff of smoke, shouts then screams, and the guard was on the ground coughing up blood. Several other guards abandoned their posts for the chance to fire their musket upon the fool, none seeming to care about the panicked crowd. One shot opened Twinkletoes' skull in a burst of brains, blood, and bone, his knees gave way, and his dead body flopped to the ground.

People swarmed, guards gathered, and I slipped away, breathing heavily, both fleeing the disturbing scene and taking advantage of the distraction Paulus provided as his last act.

The Chapel had emptied some when attendees rushed outside to discover the fatal spectacle and thus I descended the stairs with speed, only slowing when I drew close to the circular stage at the bottom.

Upon the platform was Bishop, dressed in the same white robes as me, hunched on a cane, his skin a sickly sallow and dark hair stuck to his forehead from sweat, he croaked to the hundred-some who remained with the Chapel.

"—your Hero, my beloved father, welcomed me back into the light. He reminded me that I should be *proud* of my history, of the actions of my ancestors. When the Hero first led Yorgos into Hathur, he went not to spread the light of some distant, unreachable Creator but because he was *himself* a god. His conquest of the Zarak was a holy act, confirmation of the divine destiny of Yorgos."

"You was speakin' for the Church yesser-day," someone called out.

He hobbled across the stage and stuck out a finger. "By the grace and mercy of the benevolent and magnanimous Lord Hathur, I was forgiven. I've seen the error of my ways, so believe me when I tell you: the Church is even more corrupt than you think it is. The Holy City drowns in grain while your stores run dry!"

Panic rippled through the crowd at his invocation. "N'more food?" someone squeaked.

"That's what he said," an irate woman scowled. "The Church is keepin' it all!"

"I'll starve!" a man wailed.

Bishop's voice cracked when he raised it. "Patience! Trust in the Hero. You shall understand everything—after his performance."

Every heretical word out of his mouth is burned into my memory, like a stain I can't wipe away. Behind my mask, I was slack-jawed, and my ears rang. I could hardly believe him able to stand after his injury and mistreatment, let alone preach such heresy. While I still did not believe the sincerity of his conversion, I could no longer deny that my mentor had indeed apostatized. Whether he acted genuinely or under duress did not matter so far as the Church was concerned. He was no longer "Bishop Antonius." It occurred to me then I still didn't know his birth name.

"A testament to Lord Hathur's power of persuasion, don't you think?"

The back of my neck prickled with recognition... and fear. When I turned, my worst imaginings were confirmed. Grand Arcanist Aleister stared me down, the old man unmasked and smiling. "There's no use running or denying, child. We've been waiting for you."

Only when the Grand Arcanist was jostled from behind did I shake free of shock. The tide of the crowd had returned from outside. I used the sudden crush to duck out of sight and sidle my way down the stairs. Even with wooden lifts, I was barely over five feet tall, hardly noticeable to most as I weaved my way to the stage at the bottom, all fear burned away in a reckless blaze. I no longer knew what I hoped to achieve, only that I had to confront the man who had at different times restored and shattered my faith in the Sol Creator.

I reached the bottom at a sprint, slammed into the pit railing, and tore off the suffocating mask. "Bishop!" I shouted as Aleister's masked cultists yanked me back and restrained me.

He halted his oration, looked down, and blinked. For a moment, he seemed a child himself, caught in the midst of malfeasance.

Then he turned back to the crowd.

The wind went out of me, and my limbs fell limp and numb. Rather than escort me out of the crowded Chapel, Aleister bid his cultists drag me around the circular stage, through a gate in the railing, and down spiral steps into the pit that separated the crowded hall from the raised stage. Lanterns in sconces illuminated the transformation of the foundation of the Chapel into a cavern similar to Maggy's sanctuary beneath the graveyard. Holes honeycombed the walls, some small as a fist, others large enough to be considered tunnels. Root systems, I realized, dug up and removed. *There was a Mothertree here, once.*

They shoved me along until we reached the bottom of the cavern proper. Nearby, hulking winch operators prepared the ropes and pulleys to raise a wooden platform through a massive hole in the ceiling, a hole that led to the Chapel above our heads, while rows of silent women worked spinning wheels to fashion costumes. Next to the platform, a giant iron coffin stood upright. When we passed, it *rattled*. We were "backstage."

Several holes in the cavern were barred and turned into cages that echoed with the screams of the interred. A mute man reached from between the bars with a burnt hand when I passed. It was Amell. My jailers tossed me in the cell next to his. The walls had claw-marks.

"Leave us," Aleister said. He set his lantern down and approached me. "Your Bishop saw the light. You should be proud of him. Now is your chance."

My thoughts were like daggers cutting their way out from within. "He doesn't believe it. He's lying to you all."

Rather than agitate him as I desired, the old man shrugged. "Whether he performs willingly or under duress matters not. You nor he can excuse or gainsay his words or actions. Reason is irrelevant. *Performing* is the point. Over time, performance becomes routine, routine becomes belief, and belief is *truth*. But you already know that, don't you?" He stroked my scalp, and I recoiled. "You made them all believe, all those fools in the Church. Even me, for a time. A *girl* in the heart of the Holy City. Tell me, how did you think your little adventure would end? That they would be delighted when you were discovered or revealed yourself, that they would be humbled and penitent, that they would see the error of their ways? Oh, the naiveté of children, I adore it so. You enter this world helpless, with no concept of power or what it means to wield it, in sole possession of a resource more precious than gold: innocence."

I believed my only hope for survival was to keep this monster in man's skin talking as long as I could. "I know you took the children. I know what you *do* to them, using their blood during the lord's performances!"

Again, Aleister was unperturbed. "So? Those whose families can afford tribute are spared, while the peasants call their missing children sacrifices necessary to ensure their continued freedom. I suppose if they did not tell themselves this lie they would have quite a painful confrontation with their inadequacy!" He cackled, a chilling sound. "Hathur shall do anything for its Hero. He could have eaten their children on stage and still they would have followed him this far—with farther still to go."

"Don't you see what you're doing is evil?"

"Believe it or not, I was innocent once too. My parents were Yorgosi sheep dedicated to your Sol Creator and thus bade me become the same. But I refused to join the flock. I was born to be a shepherd." He looked up at the ceiling, clearly imagining the mass of followers in the Chapel, and grinned. "Not until I ventured to Hathur did I have the veil pulled from my eyes, for I witnessed the Hero's conquest of the Zarak. He gave no mercy, no quarter. He spared no man, woman, or child. He spat at entreaties and offered no concessions. He permitted no will to exist other than his own. But most admirably, he took the Zarak children, kept some as hostages, and had the rest adopted and raised Yorgosi. He tore Hathur up by the roots and replanted the land with his seed. I was *entranced*. A vessel like the Hero makes all possible. We can march on the Holy City, seize the Church, even take Yorgos from its pathetic excuse for a king. The Pale King shall reign at last, as is our birthright."

"You're no shepherd, but a wolf. Your Pale King takes our Creator's greatest gifts and devours them. You're killing the future!"

Aleister threw back his head and hacked up more laughter. "What investment does an old man have in the future? My interest is purely in the present." The moment I dreaded came, and he drew closer to me, a hungry look on his wrinkled face. "You're a tad old for my taste, but I think we can make do..."

I scrambled away until I was curled up against the wall, frozen in fear as the so-called Grand Arcanist leaned down, breathing heavily. His bony fingers brushed my cheek and made me want to vomit. I closed my eyes... then I heard the cell door being opened. Aleister made a sound between a hiccup and a cough, and suddenly his hand withdrew. I chanced to peek.

That was when I first laid eyes on the Hero himself.

Lord Cassius Hathur had been ever-present in my mind from the time I was born there to my ignominious return, and the image I pictured was always the same: a towering man in his fifties who remained as fit as he was in his youthful prime, a soldier who wore armor at all times, an implacable lord fit for his legend. The picture held sway my entire life, as the times my father allowed me outside, I could only glimpse him from a distance during the rare times he mingled among the townsfolk. The image was so pervasive that, in that terrifying moment, I swear I *saw* such a figure standing in the doorway, framed by the faint light of the fires in the cavern beyond.

If the man who stepped within the extended glow of Aleister's lantern was ever robust and handsome, that time was *long* gone. He was almost as wide as he was tall, his unblemished armor, inlay with white enamel, strained against the bloat, bulging in the gaps between plates, and floppy golden curls were combed to cover his encroaching baldness. Caked in thick makeup, his round face was pale white save for beady blue eyes and bright red lips.

My bafflement was eclipsed by an even uglier sight: Bishop accompanied him.

I looked from the lord to my former mentor, who wore the same cowed, ashamed look he'd given when I confronted him in the Chapel, only now there was no crowd to distract him. Seeing my mentor powerless in the presence of his own father left me empty and hopeless. I'd traveled from Hathur to the Holy City and back and *nothing had changed*.

"M-my lord, apologies," Aleister stammered while he backed away and bowed profusely. "I did not expect you quite so soon."

Lord Hathur ignored his servant, hiked up the white dress he wore, and bent down to address me. "Your name is Faron," he said, as if he were the one informing me. "Aleister tells me you were sent aboard the sinking ship besmirching my harbor, that it was in fact the ship the Church sent against me. Four Shooting Stars accompanied you to investigate, four capable soldiers. Tell me why a crossdressing child like you managed to return alone?"

I stared back defiantly, not at the lord but at Bishop, wondering what roiled behind his blank mask. Had he already known that I was a girl? Had he kept my secret all these years, or was he just as ignorant as everyone else? So much would change if I knew the answer. But I never shall.

"Don't look at him," Lord Hathur commanded. "Look at me."

I was caught between trained deference and bemused revulsion. I glared at him and threw caution aside with my next words: "You look like a clown."

Aleister grabbed my ear and twisted. "Watch your tongue in front of your savior."

Lord Hathur looked down on me. "What does that make you, girl? Your kind is forbidden in the Holy City by the very Church you serve."

"The Church has burned people at stake for less!" Aleister grinned.

I implored Bishop silently, pleading with my eyes. Rather than keep my gaze, he bent his head and closed his eyes, as if in prayer. With tears welling, I'm ashamed to say I begged, "Bishop, please, help me..."

"There's no Bishop here," Lord Hathur said then prodded his son. "*Is there?*"

Bishop's blue eyes were scrunched and sorrowful. "My name is Cassius Hathur, like my father before me."

I can't explain what came over me next. It's said the Sol Creator created humans to rule over all other creatures, that we were to be as superior to beasts as our god was to us. But I know no description other than to say an *animal* inside me was loosed, and all sense of civility fell away in a primal rush of rage and wrath. I wrenched my ear from Aleister's bony grip, leapt at the crippled Bishop, and attempted to claw his eyes out. He tumbled backward in surprise, hands over his face, and I kneeled on his chest, clawing and screaming, "Liar!" over and over again. Calling him the only title that kept the pain of his betrayal at bay. Lord Cassius Hathur, the so-called Hero. His eldest son, Cassius Hathur. *Bishop*. Father twisting child into a warped reflection, destroying everything they were or could be in the process. The lord's guardsmen tore me away, thrashing and snarling, as my captors tied my hands behind my back.

I heard Lord Hathur chuckling, then his men forced me onto my knees and his pasty face loomed in mine. "The only reason you're still alive is because my namesake demanded it and you give him claw-marks as a reward. This is why mercy is for fools."

When he said "fools," I remembered Maggy saying the word too, only her fools were the holy men and women who Lord Hathur ignorantly appropriated and twisted to suit his ends. *She was right*, I thought. *She saw Bishop clearer than I ever could. Why didn't I listen?*

The lord eclipsed the fallen Bishop like a round fleshy moon. "My bastard tells me you're from Hathur, Faron. If that's true, then you must have heard of the Zarak, yes? What you don't know is that they painted their faces like this during festivals to celebrate divine authority. I once attended such celebration under the guise of diplomacy. I witnessed their holiest being treated as gods on earth. During the festival, their every demand had to be fulfilled, their every whim satisfied, and every decree obeyed. Then they began to worship *me*."

He was absolutely serious. I remember thinking, *They weren't celebrating divine authority. They were mocking kings—and you!*

"In Yorgos, there can *only* be the Sol Creator," he continued. "The One and Only, He from whence all else flowed, the all-loving sky father. The Church would have you believe I conquered Hathur because He ordained my conquest and thus it was right and just. But your priesthood did not fight the wars here. *I* did. There was no invisible hand at play, no holy destiny or grand design to the carnage, no sense to the madness at all. When a Zarak I captured told me of the deadlights, finally I understood: either an all-loving Creator does not exist—or He is not all-loving. He is malevolent. Vindictive. Judgmental. Merciless. The deadlights. The Pale King."

He was trying to scare me into obedience, just like when my father instilled his "lessons." "Why are you telling me this?" was all I could manage.

He snapped his fingers, waited while hidden servants produced a chair for him to sit in, sat, and leaned in close, his voice almost a whisper. "Because, according to both my bastard and a survivor from that ship of yours, *you've seen Him*."

I froze, afraid to confirm or deny.

"Come now, a young girl did not kill three armed soldiers by herself," Lord Hathur said. "Tell me, did He come with the midday sun?"

My pause seemed to last forever, but I finally nodded. "Everything on the ship was so bright, all I could catch were glimpses and... and the *sounds*..." I shuddered.

The lord's red lips were wet and smacked as he talked. "Do you know what it means to behold the Pale King? It means you've *sacrificed to Him*." He didn't even wait for me to deny before asking his next question. "Why did you leave Hathur for the Holy City?"

Like Bishop, I turned my gaze to the ground in shame. "I left because my father died."

He raised an eyebrow. "Of course, the town blacksmith, and how did he die?"

I was caught off-guard by his foreknowledge. "He—he drank too much. His apprentice found him surrounded by bottles, burnt up in the furnace. They said he must have slipped."

He clicked his tongue. "For a girl child, you have more balls than my full-grown bastard here. Don't be ashamed and lie to my face. Just admit the truth."

"I *am* telling the truth," I said through gritted teeth and searing tears.

"Nothing in Hathur escapes my notice, girl. *I know who you are.* You didn't leave here because your father died. You fled because you *killed* him."

I denied the charge because of course I did, but there's no reason to transcribe denials that you and I both know are lies. This tale is not just for Bishop's sake but my own. This is my confession.

My father would come home, stinking drunk, blaming me for my mother's death, and drag me into the smithy. On nights like those, I'd be lucky to escape with mere bruises. Other times, he demanded I act like I was my mother, to perform her wifely duties. I refuse to dictate those occasions. At the time, I knew no world beyond the bounds of our home and smithy. My father might as well have been the only man in the world, and in some twisted way, I still loved him. Only when I first began to sneak out, to discover Hathur beyond the walls, did my eyes open. I snuck into the old Church chapel and prayed for the first time to the Sol Creator, for the first time learning of a Creator who loved me, who could forgive and accept me, who *deserved* my love. Still, I did not act. The night I killed him was like any other drunken evening, save for one detail—his apprentice Mikkel was working late in the smithy. He claimed I let him in, called me a whore, and beat me like he never had before while Mikkel whimpered in a corner. My father growled that he and I needed to "remember who was man of the house" and dragged me to the furnace. I think he meant to brand me, but I'll never know for sure. I didn't wait to find out. I don't think he realized he brought me within reach of his tools, namely his hammers. I smashed his knee with a terrible crack, and my father screamed as he never had before. He twisted, fell, and landed in the mouth of the roaring furnace. I remember him, immobile and howling, reaching out for me. I realized what I'd done and tried to pull him out. But Mikkel stopped cowering then. He held me back, made me watch my father burn to a crisp in front of my eyes. The smithy was his from now on, he said, and if I wanted to live, I'd leave Hathur and never look back.

"The apprentice offered you up at the mere mention of torture," Lord Hathur told me after. "Worry not, I sent him to the dungeons anyway. Torturers need practice, too."

Tears streamed down my cheeks. Bishop knew everything. I had no more secrets left to give. I no longer blamed him for his betrayal. Misery directed my thoughts. *This is what I deserve. I brought it on myself.*

Lord Hathur insisted otherwise. "You should be proud you're a killer! Do you know how rare that's become since the wars ended? We might be the only two in this cell. None of my brood would dare do to me what you did to your father. They all lack the instinct, and I respect them less for it. I would have to kill them if they tried, of course, but I would like to see the effort."

His disdain roused Bishop from dull servility. "I'm not a killer."

"We shall see after tonight." Lord Hathur rose from his seat. "She is coming with us."

The younger Cassius Hathur took a step back in horror. "You said you'd spare her."

"Whether she comes to harm is your choice."

"I've done *everything* you asked," he said, pointing a finger at his father. "You *promised* if I abased myself, if I renounced the Sol Creator, you would put a *stop* to this madness."

Lord Hathur chuckled. "So gullible. Must come from his mother. If I didn't know better, I'd wonder if she passed off another Zarak babe as my issue."

Bishop, composed, patient, determined Bishop, became a child named Cassius again before my eyes. "No, I won't do it, father. I won't!"

"As I said, that is your choice. Unless you want me to kill her *now*?"

He gestured at the open cell door, the guards yanked me to my feet, and Aleister gave me a petulant push outside, though not before he whispered in my ear. "You are experiencing a great honor. Act like it and *smile*." I wished I had tried to claw *his* eyes out.

I didn't realize how drenched in cold sweat I was until I was close to the heat of the fire roaring by the winch operators and their massive platform. When Lord Hathur, Aleister, Bishop, myself, and four guardsmen in white robes wielding muskets loaded atop it, the operators whipped a pair of donkeys to rotate a massive turnstile that began our ascent.

The closer death came, the less real it seemed. I cannot otherwise account for my calmness on that rickety rise. "How does performing a play while killing children save the kingdom?" I asked.

To my amazement, he did not deny or evade the accusation. On the contrary, he was *proud*. "I'll tell you what I told my bastard: *all* of Yorgos is a performance. We like to pretend we've crawled out of the bloody muck, but we never really left. Deep down in each one of us is a beast waiting to be loosed. Like yours was when you attacked my bastard. He claimed you were pure as winter snow. But I knew the truth. Even before I knew who you were, *I knew*." He reproached the sickly Bishop with an exaggerated eyebrow. "He sees only the best in people, save the man who sired him. That is precisely what blinds him. He could not see that you are *not* pure—and a kinslayer no less! Blood against blood; no greater taboo exists. Did you know our ancestors practiced child sacrifice? The first followers of Sol offered their children to His flames. They knew innocence was the most powerful offering. From those sacrifices, the kingdom of Yorgos bloomed. Now, the practice is denied and forgotten while famine and death reign. The Church would like you to believe a child starving to death is Creator-blessed, but a child sacrificed for greatness is barbarous. What is the difference? I'll tell you: the first death is wasted."

"What did you do to them?" I was really asking, *What's going to happen to me?*

In the ascendant dark, Lord Hathur's white face seemed to glow, his red lips spread in a thin smile. Then the wooden ceiling above our heads parted, each half-circle pulled by the stagehands above, and the sudden brightness made me shut my stinging eyes.

When I opened them, I was behind the curtain. We were on stage.

Part V

The Play

The Hero, it must be said, committed no crime. Whatever occurred that tragic night of his final performance, the error could only have been his children's, his servants' or due to enemy sabotage, for never in his life was the Hero recorded to have done anything wrong. That said...

-From the official records of the Sol Church, dictated by Archbishop Claudius

---

The curtain parted on the sea of faces within the Chapel—some masked and some not—shouting deafening cheers that may as well have been all of Yorgos for how *loud* they were. If my hands hadn't been bound, I would have clapped them over my ears. The four guardsmen fanned out, Aleister shoved me forward hard enough I almost fell into the white suit of armor on display in the center, and Lord

Hathur and his namesake followed. The former basked in adulation longer than I care to recall, arms raised in triumph while the latter shrunk behind him. An eternity seemed to pass before he called for quiet.

"Many of you have attended more than one of my performances, and some attended all of them. You have been my secret keepers, ensuring that my message may be received without intermediary, give or a take a penny-pinching priest and his page." Laughter rippled while he gestured at Bishop, stooped on a cane and sweating profusely, and myself, bound and beaten. "But previous renditions were but mere rehearsals. Tonight, my friends, the performance is *real*. To you, my most faithful, I dedicate this, the final production of '*The Mystery of the Pale King.*'"

Cacophony broke at his confirmation. Again, he wallowed in the crowd's pique before giving signals to stagehands to close the curtains.

"Prepare Act I," Lord Hathur barked.

From above unrolled a tapestry depicting familiar spires hiding behind imposing walls. The background was *the Holy City*. Dozens of masked performers costumed in ostentatious yellow garb reminiscent of Church robes marched onto stage from the stairs I'd descended earlier.

Quickly, I was lost in the crush, until suddenly my arm was yanked near out of its socket. The hand belonged to Bishop. At last, his eyes were open, dark pools that I steeled myself against. "How could you give in to him?" I demanded. "This isn't you!"

His words were cold. "You knew a man named Bishop Antonius. A mask like those worn here. I was born Cassius Hathur. I cannot run from the blood in my veins. The best I can do is fight from the inside. I may never be the heir he wants me to be, but at least I can be a better lord than him. If I must suffer in apostasy until he dies, so be it."

"The Church sent you here to kill him. Now you're going to sit and wait for him to die?"

"We both agree the Church is corrupt beyond repair. Their bungling attempt to force me to assassinate my own father is proof of that. I shall not let them use me any longer."

"But you shall echo your father's heresy?"

"I suppose you would have me kill him as you did yours."

My body seemed to shrink in tandem with my voice. "Bishop, you *know* me."

"I knew an innocent boy named Faron. You are a girl who killed her father. We don't know anyone, child."

He pulled me to the wing while the cast took their marks in pairs. When the curtain parted to applause, the dreaded play began unexpectedly... with a dance.

The masked pairs spun, twirled, and leapt in unison like synchronized bumblebees, all careful to avoid the hatchway to the lift. Stagehands crawled on hands and knees to open the doors, and once more Lord Hathur rose, his back to the audience. He kicked one of the stagehands in the face when he turned around and began to walk among the couples like a ghost.

"What is a great man? Does he descend from greatness? Is he simply born that way? Or must he *become* great? I wrestled with these questions my whole life. I was born without a house name, my father's an unending line of Church piety that dates back to the Seven Solara. So naturally, I was expected to follow in their footsteps. And, if I had, I would have enjoyed a safe and comfortable life in the Holy City. As soon as I was of age, I made my pilgrimage there for initiation. I expected to find heaven on earth. Do you know what I found instead?"

He snapped his fingers.

All at once, the faceless couples shed their robes, descended to the floor, embracing, kissing, rubbing, and finally *fucking*, a moaning mass of intertwined bodies that the paunchy lord stepped over.

"A den of iniquity! They were everything they preached against, as were their followers. Look at this wanton." He grabbed a woman by the chin and smashed his mouth against hers in what looked like a painful kiss, then threw her back into the pile, his makeup smeared on her face. "Away from me, slattern!"

The audience gasped, booed, and jeered, aroused and ashamed in equal measure. For my part, I had seen male parts entirely too many times during my service as a page in the Holy City and fancied myself as rather inured to nudity in general. But when you see an orgy for the first time, curious desires awaken in you, desires you never knew you had, and suddenly you cannot see beyond them, as if a thick fog descended on my thoughts. It was only after the lord's monologue resumed that I realized more than an hour had passed.

"If this is the conduct of the highest of the land, what difference exists between those born low or high?" the Lord shouted. "None! What difference exists between evil and good? Between man and beast? None! Nature laughs at the Church's moral pretentions, harshly enforced but never obeyed. Theirs is a hatred cloaked in righteousness, a hatred of men and our rightful place in the world. Any constraint or limit placed upon us is a violation. Those like the Church who try to do so must be enemies to be treated without pity, mercy, care, or compassion. Such traits do not win wars, as I soon discovered in a distant land I barely knew, a land I would later name my own house after."

The naked performers bore Lord Hathur off-stage like royalty. The curtain closed, unseen hands rolled up the Holy City tapestry and in its place unveiled a facsimile of the very land we stood upon. Rather than a barren land and a garish town painted white, trees with leafy heads of vibrant green were numerous, the Queen's River was blue instead of brown, and the night sky made me think of the *Imantaji* painted by Maggy's people.

The curtains re-opened, and Lord Hathur marched out to more applause. "I escaped as far as I could from the Holy City, so far that I woke up one day and discovered I had left Yorgos behind entirely. I'd traveled to a place for which we had no name. The home of the Zarak."

In both wings, I witnessed the performers exchange their white masks and robes for black versions before returning to the stage. Several bore a smoking cauldron I recognized all too well. They set it down and danced around it in an ugly pantomime of the ceremony I'd witnessed underground. One by one, they reached within, withdrew and displayed obsidian stones.

"I observed their customs, spoke with their priests, and participated in their ceremonies. They respected me so much that I became the first Yorgosi to undertake their holiest rite." Then Lord Hathur himself seized a smoking stone with a gloved hand. "*And I was not burned.*"

While the crowd roared its approval, I could only gape and hold my burnt right hand. I remembered the ease with which the *Imantaji* grasped the rocks, the way they proffered them to others including children: in their ritual, theirs must not burn *at all*. The absolute power their performance mocked, the ignorant "Hero" believed in without reservation.

Worse, so did his audience.

"I returned to Yorgos a changed man," the lord continued. "But rather than honor their prodigal son, the Church branded me a traitor and a heretic, slanders they continue to this day. They would have executed me then, but with the people behind me, they knew I was right and they were wrong. Then, as now, *they* are the traitors. *They* are the heretics!"

The would-be Zarak lined up on either side of him, forming a path from the cauldron to the front of the stage, and knelt when he passed. "I defied the Church's edicts and returned to this very land we stand upon, my purpose finally clear. The Holy City was a prison, a tomb for my greatness, one that I just barely escaped. Here, I could be the god I was always meant to be."

I watched another litany of performers in white robes and bladed muskets charge out of the opposite wing and clash with their black counterparts on stage. Over the next hour, Lord Hathur detailed his version of history, wherein he was a flawless military genius with courage and cunning none could match. To hear him tell it, he led each battle from the frontlines and personally assassinated several enemy leaders.

"Nobody can possibly believe this," I muttered, unable to hide my disdain.

Bishop cut me to the quick. "You did, not two days ago. Now quiet. Your role approaches."

Several performers wheeled out an upright iron coffin, the front molded to portray a man in agony. My heart hammered in my chest. "What is that? What role?"

"You're me," he replied. "Just remember: your mark is on top of the hatchway."

"I'm you? Please, Bishop, I trusted you. Why won't you tell me what's happening? Why are you making me do this?"

He looked at me with haunted eyes. "Sacrifice is never easy. Else, it is not sacrifice."

"Then I came upon a *child*," Lord Hathur called shrilly from stage, breaching the wall of terror within me.

Bishop gave me a light push, and I stumbled out onto the stage, a thousand eyes on me. Many of the performers lay on the ground in piles of would-be corpses, the result of the lord's war reenactments. The lord himself jerked his head at the hatchway. The iron coffin rattled when I passed again. Whatever was inside wanted out.

I wobbled on my mark, more and more certain that I was about to die. Was this the fate that befell Hathur's children? Props for the lord's theatrics?

"A child, all alone in the aftermath of battle," the lord droned on as he drew closer, "hiding by the shores of the Queen's River. Our enemies were known to use children as weapons so I approached this child with grim belief, prepared to do what must be done." His sweaty bloated body loomed over me then and he shoved me to the right. I'd forgotten how to breathe.

Then a trapdoor opened beneath me, and I left my stomach behind, plummeting...

...five feet onto the platform we'd ridden to the stage.

Stagehands splashed me with water, soaking me to the bone, before they dragged me to my feet. I blinked away water and stared with disbelief. Dozens of giggling children surrounded me, many even younger than I was.

"Is it scary up there?" a small boy squeaked. "We practiced hard to not disappoint him!"

I couldn't form words. Hathur's children, white-faced and red-lipped like their lord, and waiting to participate in his performance. He hadn't killed them, not all at least. He held them for tonight. Above our heads, one of the lord's stubbly hands reached down. A woman lifted my arm, put my hand in his, then he yanked hard, and he pulled me back out of the trapdoor like a sack of flour.

"Behold! The power to take life *and* give it. After I saved the child from drowning, he thanked me and called me his hero." He squeezed my shoulder, beady blue eyes boring holes into me.

"Th-thank you, my lord." He squeezed tighter. "You're my hero."

"Those who witnessed the incident heard his words, and henceforth I was known as the Hero of Hathur!" He raised his other arm high and absorbed the crowd's rapturous response.

"Now, my friends," he continued. "I promised you truth tonight, and I'm a man of my word. Many here have missing children, some given, some taken, but all treated with the care your progeny deserve. They have lived with me in my castle for some time, learned at my feet, and prepared for this night almost as much as I did. Your faith has been rewarded. I have performed a miracle: your children, returned to you!"

The hatchway opened, the platform rose, and gasps and cries of relief echoed from the parents in the audience. The children poured out, grabbed muskets and pistols off the "corpses" and started to march in circles around the lord with stiff arms and rigid steps shouting "Hathur, Hathur, Hathur!" The curtain closed without the children returning to their parents.

Once hidden, the lord's smile vanished. "Clear the stage! Prepare the final act! And you!" he shouted at me, "Bring me my bastard."

"No need, father," Bishop said as he passed the armed children. Seeing him triggered understanding of his earlier words. *My role was him. What we performed really happened.*

Lord Hathur confirmed my suspicion. "How did it feel to watch your own experience?"

"That wasn't my experience," Bishop said. "I dove into the river to escape you, not by some accident. You didn't save me; then as now, you captured me."

"Protest all you like, we both know you ran because were a bastard who would never inherit. If you had ever stood to gain, you would have turned out no different than your siblings."

"I suppose it's lucky for you they're around." His eyes narrowed. "Where are they?"

He waved an indifferent hand. "Drusus and Livia chose to be witless sycophants. Julius broke rather than bent. Are you strong enough to do what they failed to?" He pointed at me. "She is the last obstacle on your path to redemption, the last cord you must cut to become a free man. If you do what is necessary, you shall inherit all Hathur upon my ascension tonight. If you can't even kill to survive, then let her kill you, for both our sakes."

Bishop blinked back utter surprise. The iron coffin rattled again. "What did you do...?"

"I'm giving you what you always wanted. What happens now is your choice."

"No, this is *your* choice, as always, forced upon us!"

He strutted next to his shrunken son. "When hungry wolves devour a flock of sheep, do you blame the wolves? Or the shepherd who failed to protect his flock?" He grabbed Bishop by the nape of his neck. "The shepherd you cling to, this sky father you seek to replace me with, where is He? When has the Sol Creator ever stopped me from doing whatever I want, whenever I want to? I'll tell you: not once. The idea that He—or any god—is above me in any way is *absurd*. And in the final act, I shall prove it to you. Aleister! Is our tribute prepared?"

The old man mingled among the children, the only one smiling, when he snapped to attention. "Indeed, my lord! All of history has led to this night. Your ascent to godhood shall bring about the return of Yorgos' glorious past. Our acolytes stand above our heads, pouring tribute as we speak."

Pouring? Pouring what? I turned to Bishop in dismay but found him focused on his father with a blank, stony rage that frightened me further. Lord Hathur stared back with equal intensity. "Are you tired of being a bastard?"

The Bishop I knew would never consider Lord Hathur's offer, but I had never really known the man, not even his true name. My faith shattered, it was suddenly so easy to see his ambition within the Church as a substitute for what his father had denied him. If he was willing to follow his father this far, why wouldn't he do as he bid now? Bishop had betrayed me over and over to my face. My only other option was death. *I'm a killer and he's not.* Thoughts that once filled me with righteous anger now fill me with shame. Age condemns us all.

"If I'm to do this, you must do something for me." Bishop pointed at Aleister. "The Grand Arcanist plots against me and thus you. If I am to be your heir, he must die."

Aleister threw back his wrinkly head and cackled. "You show your treasonous hand by smearing me with lies. I've worshipped the Pale King before you were a curse upon your holy father. I would sacrifice anything for my lord, unlike you who spurned his godly gifts by absconding to the Church. Your slander condemns you, bastard."

Lord Hathur gestured at his four guardsmen. "Kill the Grand Arcanist."

Even Bishop seemed surprised by the ease with which he gave the order. The old man's laughter died on the spot. "My lord," he sputtered, "you can't possibly believe— I've been nothing but loyal."

He nodded at him serenely. "That's why this is so difficult for me. I would personally never die for anyone, yet here you are, about to die for me willingly. A shame you can only honor me once." The guards closed in on the shrieking Aleister, bladed muskets pointed at him, when the lord gave an uncharacteristic sigh and called, "Halt! I cannot kill my friend like this."

His capriciousness gave me whiplash. Aleister wiped his runny nose, a smile of relief revealing every wrinkle on his face. "Thank you, my lord, your mercy is divine!"

The lord waved the children over. "Would you like the honor of killing my friend?"

They all looked at each other, nervous and wary, before grinning and nodding eagerly.

"The young eat the old," Lord Hathur noted dryly, ordered the protesting Aleister gagged and restrained, and placed me and Bishop on either side of the iron coffin, under watch. The background changed for the last time, a tapestry of Hathur as it stood: identical, white, sterile.

"Are you really going to try and kill me?" I asked Bishop, making what passed for threats from me. "I mean, I've killed before, and you haven't. Don't—don't think I won't do it if you make me."

"Proud of patricide now, are you?" he said out of the corner of his mouth.

"The world would be better if you were!"

"Have I taught you nothing, Faron?" he hissed. "We are *not* gods. Life and death is the domain of the Sol Creator, and it is to His hands I entrust my fate, as should you."

I looked at him incredulously. "The Church sent you here to *kill* him, or did you forget? What you've taught me is that I can't trust anyone, not even the Sol Creator! He hasn't done *anything*, Bishop! He lets it all happen, and all you ever have are empty words. If He cared about us, we wouldn't be here, on stage, about to—" I couldn't finish my sentence and instead said something I knew would cut him deepest. "Either our Creator doesn't care, or *He doesn't exist.*"

As if in answer, the curtain opened to rabid cheers. Lord Hathur absorbed them as he had every time, then directed their gaze to the terrified Aleister. "Our Grand Arcanist attempted to kill me. I call upon your judgment, my beloved followers: how should we reward this traitor?"

"DEATH!" the crowd roared without hesitation.

"I am beholden to my people." He flicked his wrist.

The guards threw the blubbering Aleister on the ground while the children descended and turned the old man into a bloody pincushion not ten feet in front of us. Muted shock tempered the crowd's first reaction save the most reverent, a cohort which swelled when Lord Hathur feted the children for their violent obeisance.

Detestable as Aleister was, I couldn't help but seethe at Bishop. "*You* did that. They're as bad as me now, thanks to you. None of *us* ever had a choice!"

He said nothing. I wonder if he agreed with me.

Lord Hathur praised the children and promised them new lives as his acolytes. The deafening roars of approval returned and encompassed almost all who had refrained during the execution. He began another monotonous monologue when a boy vomited on stage. He berated the crying child, snatched the musket from his tiny hands, and ordered his guards to usher the gaggle of children (and Aleister's corpse) off-stage.

"What was I saying?" The audience laughed. "Ah yes, I conquered Hathur single-handedly and then—"

"The deadlights!" someone in the crowd yelled with glee. "You saw the deadlights!"

"That's right." His crimson lips curved. "And tonight, so shall all of you."

There were surprised gasps, fearful yelps, and rampant praise. Far in the back, I saw a few attendees attempt to leave, only to be stopped by masked cultists.

The lord stalked the stage like a predator did its prey. "When the war ended, the Church demanded I return to the Holy City and seek absolution for my so-called sins, but I refused. I was *compelled* to stay, compelled to disobey and seek the truth behind a Zarak legend."

As many as a hundred performers in black robes rushed onstage from the wings, Lord Hathur a stark contrast as the sole white figure amongst them, though a few others wore identical white makeup and painted their lips red. The dance went on and on and on in arrhythmic fashion around these few, to whom the rest bowed. I was watching either a mockery or poor imitation of the ritual I'd witnessed underground.

"He's getting it all wrong!" The point of a musket poked my back, an unwelcome reminder of the leering guard behind me.

"In the smoking mountains of Hathur," he began, "dwells a light so intense it drives men mad to look upon it, a power they named the *deadlights*. Despite the blazing suns on our banners, the Zarak claimed we worshipped not the Sol Creator, but these deadlights. Of course, what could I do then but laugh. Until the war. Countless of my men vanished in these very forests, well before we chopped them down. The survivors we found, which weren't many, were all blind, bloody, and gibbering about being swallowed by light. Men cowered in fear, some blaming native curses and others the Sol Creator's displeasure. I sought the deadlights to dispel such outlandish rumors—that is, until I witnessed them myself. Every single man in my company died or worse that fateful night—except me. I alone survived the deadlights untouched, empowered even. I could not stop asking: why had I been spared while all others suffered terrible fates?

"The mystery persisted until I summoned my dear friend Aleister to court," Lord Hathur gestured at bloodstains left by his 'dear friend.' "He first told me the tale immortalized by me. Long before Yorgos, there lived a prince, the largest and strongest of the royal brood. But alas, he was not the eldest and thus far down the line of succession. He stood to inherit a pittance, unless his elder siblings died first. Then they did. One by one, brothers and sisters alike died in horrible accidents and misfortunes, until he was the eldest yet living. But his king father and younger siblings knew this prince had a hand in the deaths and vowed to disinherit him. The prince was left with no choice. He killed his father and younger siblings too. His familial sacrifices made him the first vessel for the deadlights: *the Pale King*. A cautionary tale others said, a warning to be heeded. But all I could think when I heard the tale was what *brilliance*, what purity of purpose, to sacrifice *everything* for glory. At last, I understood what I must do."

He unfurled his arm, drawing attention to the iron coffin between me and Bishop. The crowd roared with a breathless anticipation that indicated they knew not what came next or thought they did. Did they truly endorse his slavering for savagery, or were they simply ignorant to the evil lurking beneath the performance? A distinction without difference. The result was the same. Still, I can't help but wonder if the purpose of the lord's previous performances—"rehearsals" he called them—had been to inure townsfolk for the bloodshed to come.

"Faron, *look away*," Bishop croaked. Sicklier than ever, hair stuck to his sweaty forehead, he hunched over to me on his cane, near the brink of collapse, but stagehands brushed us apart and heaved the thick coffin door open. Of course, just like everyone else, I looked.

Crawling out of the coffin on four spindly limbs and draped in bloody animal pelts was a creature so pale its exposed skin was translucent, its face featureless thanks to the blank white mask strapped to its face—the same beast I had glimpsed in the woods of Hathur and believed only I could see. The stage put a stake through that belief, the appearance welcomed by the audience rather than reviled, for the lord had unveiled the creature before, perhaps at every performance. Questions clouded my mind, and I instinctively looked toward Bishop for guidance. But his wide gaze was locked on the open coffin and the horror yet within.

Impaled on the many spikes that lined the innards of the coffin were a near-identical man and woman, naked and so pale as to be bloodless, dead blue eyes staring outward.

Drusus and Livia Hathur, his eldest children.

"To be human is to be weak," Lord Hathur declared to the oblivious crowd. "The Pale King must cease to be human, inside and out. Only when he sacrifices the sacred does he become a *god*." He stared proudly at the bodies in the coffin. "There is nothing more sacred than youth."

The guards finally took their eyes off me to warily surround the beast, which sniffed the air from behind its mask then, as if the guards weren't even there, bounded around them to leap at an unsuspecting Bishop, bringing him to the ground and snarling in my former mentor's face. Without thinking, I rushed to his aide while the listless guards dithered about, grabbed the creature by the head, and pulled as hard as I could, forgetting that my right hand remained a burnt mess. My grip slipped, I fell, and I grabbed the straps of its mask, pulling it off in the process.

Beneath, single strands of stringy white hair clung to its paper-thin scalp, its teeth and chin blood stained, and it was missing lips, both ears, and its nose. But its *eyes*, its eyes were blue, blue like Bishop's.

Bishop looked up, not with fear but recognition—and grief. "Julius?" he whispered.

The thing that had been Julius Hathur snarled in response, either a dismissal or a threat. Lord Hathur snapped his fingers, and his son bounded to his side like a hound might.

"Behold, a portrait of the unworthy!" I thought he spoke of the deformed offspring by his side but rather he pointed a stubby finger at us. "The Church brands me pagan, but *they* are the true pagans! The hypocrites have fallen so far as to send mine own bastard to kill me, alongside, of all things, a girl pretending to be a boy."

The audience grew particularly vitriolic, as if my supposed transgression was the most heinous of the night.

"They do not realize the truth," Lord Hathur concluded. "The Pale King *is* their Sol Creator, the eternal brightness we leave when we are born and return to when we die, and He and I share a name, the same as my land, my castle, and my blood. *Hathur.* Praise Hathur! Praise me!"

Besotted by his bloody promises, they did. "Hathur! Hathur! Hathur!"

"Lift your eyes to the heavens!" he raised his arms in ecstasy. "The paradise of the Pale King, *my paradise*, answers my call. I alone have made it real!"

Through the skylight, a phantom city of a thousand different architectures swallowed the stars, vacant ruins from another time or place. Everyone was looking up in awe, the audience, the performers, the lord's guards, including the nearest one whose musket drooped in one hand. I seized my chance—and his musket.

Heavy and awkward in my arms, I swayed and balanced on time bought by the distracted soldier's shock, shoved the butt into my shoulder, aimed at Lord Hathur, and fired.

The crack of the musket was ear-splitting, and gunpowder smoke stung my nostrils, but I could still see the thing that had been Julius

Hathur leap in front of his father to take the shot. His body was so thin and frail that the impact opened up his chest like the coffin he'd emerged from.

I was disarmed and face down on the ground soon enough, left to stare across the floor of the stage at the mutilated face of the second man I'd killed. Frankly, I gave the poor man mercy.

Rather than rage at me or mourn his son, he snarled at Bishop, "The girl is more man than you! You're a parasite, just like your siblings. If you're not careful, you'll share their fate. The time has come to perform your role. There's no way off this stage without killing or dying." He snatched a musket from a guard and handed it to Bishop. "Time to grow some balls."

Bishop's eyes drifted from his father to the phantom city above our head, and finally landed on the gun, which he accepted with shaking hands. Lord Hathur guided his last, sickly son across the stage to where I was pinned against the ground. The quivering point of the musket blade hovered inches from my cheek. I glared up the barrel at the man I knew as Bishop with every ounce of wrath and disdain I had within. If he was going to kill me, he would have to look me in the eyes. Tears leaked out of his.

Then he swung the musket around, the pointed tip making the nearby guards leap out of the way and aimed the gun at his father. For the first time, Lord Hathur appeared scared. Bishop pulled the trigger. But this time, there was only a click.

A misfire. Of all times, a misfire.

Fear faded from Lord Hathur's garishly pale face, and he started to grin before he noticed what we all did as well. The room was getting brighter. Not the warm, comforting light cast from the flames within the braziers and lanterns but a different sort—cold, alien, and unnatural, just like the entity had been above the bleeding deck of the half-sunken *Maiden-Made-of-Light*. Collective eyes turned to the heavens.

The deadlights came from above our heads and eclipsed the phantom city beyond the skylight. Light illuminated the cracked ceiling like an incandescent spider-web, conjoined in a blazing center. Through the cracks, blood showered down like a tempest of red rain on the screaming masses packed together beneath hot oppressive stone trying desperately to escape through the narrow exits of the crumbling chapel, their white robes stained shades of scarlet. Horrid understanding struck me. *That's what the Hero ordered to be poured: blood. It came because of the blood.*

Several of the performers escaped by leaping down into the stage pit, where lay the stairs I had descended backstage earlier. I dodged falling debris and moved to join them, but once again, something within stopped me. Call it stupid, call it sentimental, call it both, I couldn't leave Bishop behind. Perhaps that's why he did what he did.

All I could see were outlines of people in the growing cascade of light, but my mentor's was unmistakable. Unlike everyone else fleeing, Bishop grappled with another, larger shadow—Lord Hathur. Their outlines warped and faded until all trace of their struggle was lost in the deadlights, but I could still hear Bishop's voice, distorted and pitched like he had no fixed position.

"I did everything you told me to do, so why did you do this? *Why?* My title, my family, my *faith*. All you do is take! Then take me!" Whether he raged against the Sol Creator or his father, I'll never know. Perhaps, for him, there was little difference.

Everything was too bright to see. Up was down. Sound sped up and slowed down. I tripped backing up and ended up on my back, blinking upward, and rather than run, I held up hand to glimpse what lay behind the deadlights.

A glowing underside of insectoid ridges and bulbous sacs pulsed with waves of light like a heartbeat, invisible limbs lapped at the brightness and sent many-colored ripples out like the light was shimmering water, and a solitary eye blinked a thousand eyelids. I don't know if it was the deadlights or the being behind them that mocked comprehension, but solidity and definition elided my senses, like trying to grip a handful of sand. What I saw could have been a beast of flesh and blood that *mimicked* light. What I perceived as wings could have been fins. What I thought of as one could be many. Indeed, the source of the deadlights seemed to come apart and back together again, as if it were not one entity but legion, a flock, a school, a *swarm*, and in its midst, held aloft by the hints of pincers and talons, the shadows Bishop and Lord Hathur fused, divided, and then disintegrated in a haze of red mist.

I'm certain I would have continued staring in blind awe until death came for me, paralyzed by an experience beyond my young imagination, had someone not grabbed my hand and pulled my listless self through the invisible maze of bluish light. Either the deadlights started to fade, or we exceeded its reach, because I soon could make out my rescuer: one of the lord's insulting 'Zarak' performers garbed in a black costume.

"Who are you?" I said, or thought I did. They ignored me in favor of pushing through the exits and passed the panicked masses ensconced in the waning deadlights. Some clawed their eyes out, others bit off the lips and tongue, and yet more attacked others to gnaw off ears and noses. When crazed congregants got in our way, my rescuer moved swiftly and knifed them in the groin or throat with icy precision.

Outside the chapel, the deadlights had risen into the sky, blood still raining down from its feast, and skipped behind a curtain of clouds like a moving lightning strike making its way back to the mountains.

Hathur, for its part, was *chaos*. Injured townsfolk in their bloodstained robes ran amuck while the seedier elements, recently drawn to Hathur like vultures or carrion, vandalized, pillaged, and ransacked at will. A fresh wave of panic came over me, and I yelled to be freed. In response, the last person I expected to be my savior removed their mask.

"Maggy?" I choked out breathlessly.

She opened her mouth to speak but another voice interrupted, detestable and familiar.

"Guards! Guards, shoot them! Where are my guards?" Against all odds, Lord Hathur stumbled out of the ruined chapel, white and red makeup smudged and smeared across his face, armor and undershirt broken and torn enough to expose his flabby belly.

I looked to Maggy and back in disbelief. "Why does he always survive?"

"Cockroaches always do," she replied.

"*I* am the god; *you* are the insect," Lord Hathur roared at us, as if he was glad for the distraction from the destruction of his family and home. His bellow left him bent over coughing.

"Where's Bishop?" I demanded. "Tell me what happened to him!"

He ignored me, beady blue eyes wide and mad. "My ritual worked! The deadlights chose me: *I* am the Pale King! Bow before your new god!"

Of what happened next, I can say only that instinct guided me once more. I seized Maggy's dagger from its sheath on her belt, yanked it free, and charged Lord Hathur. By the time his coughing fit ended and he noticed me, I was almost upon him. All he could do was flail while I sunk the blade deep into the rolls of his exposed stomach. Eyes wide, mouth agape, the man known as the Hero of Hathur could only blink at the blood gushing around the wound. Even I hesitated, overwhelmed by my own decision. Then I yanked the dagger free in a crimson spurt and plunged it in him, again and again and again, until he toppled onto the ground and took the blade with him. I pulled it free again, heard him whisper something I couldn't discern between gurgles, and drove the dagger into his throat like a stake into the ground. Head resting on the end of the hilt, I watched the disbelieving lights behind his beady blue eyes vanish.

It wasn't until she was directly behind me that I noticed Maggy had quietly approached and that I hadn't moved. I let go of the dagger and looked myself up and down, my white robes ashen, bloody, and ripped, and tried to wipe my hands clean on them to no avail.

"Do you think I'm a monster?" I asked Maggy without looking at her.

"The monster here is finally dead," she said as she removed her dagger from the dead Hero's throat, wiped it clean on his corpse and sheathed it. "You are Faron."

I sniffed a hollow laugh. "I don't know who I am anymore."

She offered me her hand. "Whoever you want to be."

Part VI

Now

With no surviving witnesses to the events therein, this inquiry is concluded. Long live King Leo of Yorgos and praise to the Sol Creator, the One and Only.

-From the official records of the Sol Church, dictated by Archbishop Claudius

---

For the sake of its so-called Hero, Yorgos destroyed itself. Some called the Hero's death a Church assassination, others a coup perpetrated by his children, and yet more claimed he had risen to the heavens on the backs of angels. Insurrection spread like a plague across Yorgos, many factions led, unsurprisingly, by mutinous Shooting Stars. King Leo died and became known as Leo the Last or simply the Last King. Rival factions vie for power now: Pale King cultists, Sol Creationists, and Maggy's people too, seizing back the lands the Yorgosi seized from them. Nobody seems to know the truth of what happened in Hathur. Except me and Maggy.

It's winter now. As I write these words, I sit in the ruined library of the Holy City. Glorious halls once full of books, acolytes, and crackling fires lays cold and empty, full of ashes and rats. The Church that had stood as the central pillar of Yorgosi life for hundreds of years was gone, and the kingdom with it. I do not mourn its passing. This tomb is a reminder that people's creations are just as mortal as our bodies. The wealthiest, strongest, or most intelligent person is destined to be forgotten, just like the rest of us. Over time, even gods may die.

I set out to write Bishop's exoneration and let go of the hurt of his betrayal. But perhaps years have withered my sympathy, for I find little peace in the writing. If anything, my account has hardened me against the man I looked at as a surrogate father. He was not a teacher but a lesson, a cautionary tale. Both men named Cassius Hathur, father and son, lord and bishop, sought to master this baffling and unyielding world or die in the attempt. Bishop entrusted his fate to the absent Sol Creator and paid the ultimate price while Lord Hathur embraced his damnation and made debasement his religion.

The world has always been baffling and unyielding to me. People who should be forgotten are immortalized while many who deserve recognition are dismissed from memory because they did not conform to a world designed by men like Bishop, Lord Hathur, and my father. For me, the Pale King is no mystery. The legend is the fearful gasp of their dying world, Yorgos destroyed by the all-consuming light of its beloved Sol Creator. But darkness? Darkness sustains. What keeps us alive lives in the darkness. Light is finite. We call what its glow chances upon 'known,' but knowledge is an illusion, what we know temporary and ever-changing. Only the unknown is eternal.

Perhaps I'm neither Faron the blacksmith's daughter from Hathur nor Faron boy page of the Church of the Sol Creator. Perhaps I'm both and *more*. Perhaps my potential is what scared everyone: my father, the priests, Bishop, the townsfolk, all the cruelty and shame rooted in jealousy, jealousy that I am free in a way they shall never be, that I can accept who I am while they remain trapped only so far as their beloved light reaches. I learned to dwell in darkness, my role in the fate of the kingdom unknown to everybody.

Almost everybody.

Maggy, you shall return soon. But I won't be here. You'll look down on my scribbled story in the empty pages of the Church's record book, read its lines until you come to this one, furious that I decided to leave, perhaps even cursing my hubris for recording the secret that marks me the Hero's killer. But you'll know as well as I that her people need her. And I need them to be safe.

I no longer feel shame about my past. I feel *pride*, Maggy. Pride in who I am, in what I've done... and what I'm going to do. Please don't destroy these words. Save them. Share them. Destroy the myth of the lone Hero, the solitary god, the One and Only. Lord Hathur was but a pretender, a would-be usurper. The deadlights remain, a pale king seated on a throne of smoke belched by eternal flame, awaiting the next fool to summon his power. It's said he can never die.

I shall put the legend to the test.

Acknowledgements

The idea of a "self-made man" is a myth, an aspirational lie. We are all products of our environments and that is particularly true of artists, as I can attest. This book would not exist without the following people:

Marty Spang for becoming my de facto editor, Martin Barnier for being my sounding board for all my craziest ideas, Alex Greenawalt for their sensitivity reading, Ryan Hill and Molly Markley, as well as Bob Satmary and the whole O'Betty's crew for their friendship and support during the writing of this story.

Sylvia Langille of Timber Ghost Press for her belief in this story and Greg Chapman for bringing the cover in my head to terrifying life.

My sister Hannah for the towering example she sets, my brother-in-law Joe for the light he shines in our lives and my newborn nephew Joey for joining the party just in time.

Dad for being the man I look up to and Mom for the heart she freely gives.

My wife Angela for her unwavering love. Without you, there is no story.

About the Author

Sam Flynn (he/him) is an author based out of Ohio. He investigates the intersections between speculative genres, the psychic spaces where dreams are reality, history bleeds horror, and mystery reigns supreme. Books were constant companions along his life journey and his greatest hope is that his writing can provide other readers the same inspiration or companionship. If he can scare you too, all the better.

You can read more about him at www.sam-flynn.com, @Samfly-nn1992 on Twitter, Instagram, and Threads, and @samflynnwrites. bsky.social on BlueSky.

A Note from Timber Ghost Press

If you enjoyed *The Mystery of the Pale King*, please consider leaving a review on Amazon or Goodreads. Reviews help the authors and the press.

If you go to www.timberghostpress.com you can sign up for our newsletter so you can stay up-to-date on all our upcoming titles, plus you'll get informed of new horror flash fiction and poetry featured on our site monthly.

Take care and thanks for reading *The Mystery of the Pale King!*

-Timber Ghost Press